James is on the run, and as if that isn't enough of a problem, he needs to find a safe place to shift. He's a new werewolf, and he's still not fully in control of his wolf, especially during the full moon. He's never hurt anyone, and he's not about to start, but that means chaining himself to a wall, or in this case, to an old sink. And that means leaving himself vulnerable for the night.

Fyfe hates being responsible for the coven, but he doesn't have a choice. He likes escaping in the last hours of the night, when the rest of the city is asleep.

Only, it's not asleep tonight.

When Fyfe stumbles onto a man beating up a werewolf, he intervenes. The wolf is chained to the wall and vulnerable, and if there's one thing Fyfe doesn't like, it's people taking advantage of the weak. He kills the assailant and helps the wolf as he shifts back to human. The fact that he takes in the wolf has nothing to do with how cute he thinks James is, of course.

But James is still on the run, and now, Fyfe has someone to protect. Fyfe isn't easily convinced, though, even when James tells him the conclave is after him. The conclave isn't going to stop, and they both know it. Is James going to have to keep on running from the conclave, or will he and Fyfe find a way to prove him innocent?

Beloved Fangs
Copyright © 2019 Catherine Lievens
ISBN: 978-1-4874-2412-1
Cover art by Angela Waters

Published by eXtasy Books Inc or
Devine Destinies, an imprint of eXtasy Books Inc

Look for us online at:
www.eXtasybooks.com or www.devinedestinies.com

Beloved Fangs
Life with Fangs Book 2

By

Catherine Lievens

CHAPTER ONE

James rubbed his face and looked at the sky. *Goddammit.* He needed to find a safe place for the night. He could already feel the ripple of the wolf inside him. It was going to come out whether James liked it or not, and James needed to be sure no one would get hurt when that happened.

Someone bumped against him. A growl escaped his lips before he could stop himself. The man didn't look afraid, although since James could smell he was human, it wasn't surprising. He didn't have a reason to fear James, not yet, not when James was still human.

But he wouldn't be human for much longer tonight.

James was tempted to go after the guy. He knew it was only because of the wolf, and he pushed back. The wolf never took disrespect well, especially from humans, and it was close to the surface tonight, so close that James was having a hard time controlling it.

But he had to.

He shuffled toward the nearest alley and took his phone out. He'd just arrived in the city, and he had no idea where to look for a safe place. It needed to be isolated and empty, and he had to be able to chain himself to something. It wasn't an easy thing to find a place that fit, but this was a city. There had to be an abandoned warehouse or building somewhere where he could spend the night. He needed to hurry, though, and he needed to make sure no one noticed him. The city was big, and there had to be other paranormal creatures around. There always were.

James wasn't supposed to stick around without finding them and contacting them, but that would only lead to his arrest and his death, so that was not an option, even though they could have helped him.

Thank God for cell phones and the internet. It took James five minutes to find out which part of the city he should look for an abandoned building in. It wasn't far, so he hurried there, his gaze never straying far from the sky. He could feel the moon in his veins, under his skin, pushing him toward the change. His body wanted to obey, but he still had a bit of time before he *had* to. He was going to fight it as hard as he needed to. He had to be off the streets before it happened. He wasn't going to hurt anyone, no matter what some people thought he'd done.

The sidewalks became emptier the deeper James walked into this area of the city. He stopped once he was alone. He wasn't afraid of what could happen to him—he was a werewolf, and even when he was human, he was stronger than most humans. He wasn't supposed to expose himself and the supernatural world, but he'd do it to defend himself if necessary. He was already being hunted anyway. It was for something he hadn't done, but adding to it wouldn't change his fate if they got him.

There was a motel at the corner of the street. James looked at it, wondering for a brief moment if he could maybe spend the night there. He knew it wasn't possible, though, so he pushed that thought away. Even if he managed to lock himself into the bathroom and make sure he wasn't able to leave in his werewolf form, there was no way he wouldn't be heard. His shift wasn't exactly inconspicuous. He'd be out of the city tomorrow morning, but in the meantime, he needed to be invisible.

So he walked on. He left the motel behind and headed toward an abandoned warehouse instead. The asphalt in the parking lot was cracked, with stray grass growing in patch-es. James could see several broken windows, so he was pret-ty sure no one had been in the warehouse in a while, at least not to work. He might have to make sure no one was using it to sleep, though. The last thing he wanted was for a home-less person to find him shifted. He wouldn't eat them like he'd been afraid he might in the beginning, but he could hurt them, or worse, and he didn't want that to happen.

The door wasn't locked. James wasn't surprised—they seldom were. He'd gotten used to haunting empty buildings since he'd started running.

The first thing he did was walk through all the rooms. A huge one occupied most of the space, but James couldn't tell what it had been used for. All the machines that should have been there had no doubt been sold, and only the imprints were left in the dust on the floor.

James didn't waste time trying to understand what they'd been for. He went to the smaller rooms, making sure no one was there. He found two locker rooms with bathrooms and what might have been a break room. None of them had had human occupants in a while, not from the smell—and James was pretty good with that. If there was one thing being a werewolf was good for, it was this. He could tell there were rats in the walls, and that another kind of animal had been around recently, maybe a feral cat, or even a possum. He knew the animals had used the men's locker room, so he went to the women's instead. It wasn't like anyone else was going to use the place tonight, so who cared?

He wanted a shower, but he knew better than try to open the water in one of the showers. Even if there was some— and it was a stretch—it would be filthy. He could go to the motel around the corner tomorrow morning once he was human again and get a room to shower, maybe even sleep for a few hours. The sooner he was out of the city, the better it would be, but he was always tired after a shift and a night spent in his furry form. He could use a good night's sleep, and it would probably help in the long run. Besides, he didn't think he'd been followed. He had no doubt the conclave enforcers would eventually track him, but he should be fine for a few days.

That motel room was looking better and better.

But first, James had stuff to do. He dropped his bag on the floor and crouched next to it. He took the chains out and dumped them next to the closest sink. He would hook them over the plumbing and hope it was more resistant than it had been when he'd done this the month before. The plumbing had given during the night, and he'd found himself in the middle of a deserted parking lot, buck ass naked, the next morning. He was lucky no one had seen him and called the cops. It would have been a massacre if they'd tried to grab him while he was in his werewolf form, and he couldn't afford to be locked up, not with the conclave always so close behind him.

James took his clothes off and pushed them into his backpack. He shivered even though the room wasn't that cold. Well, it was, but his body temperature always ran warmer than humans ever since he'd been bitten and changed. It wasn't the cold that made him shiver, though. He could feel the moon even though he couldn't see it. It slithered under his skin and pushed at the flimsy control he still had over his werewolf form. He wouldn't be able to keep it in for long, not with the moon feeling more powerful with every minute that passed.

He leaned down and grabbed the end of the chain. He'd hooked a pair of handcuffs there. It was the best he'd been able to come up with. He knew it wasn't ideal, and that he'd end up with scrapes on his wrists from trying to get the handcuffs off, but it was better than waking up in the morning with blood on his hands.

He hooked the chain around the plumbing and snapped the handcuffs shut around his wrists. He grimaced at the floor, but he sat down anyway, the broken edges of the tiles digging into his ass. He hated the thought of sitting naked on the filthy floor, but it was better than waiting standing up. It wouldn't be long anyway. Then he'd have fur, and he wouldn't care about the floor being dirty.

He just had to wait a few more minutes and give in to the pull of the moon.

Fyfe didn't want to answer the phone. He already knew who it was. The number was saved on his cell phone under Asshat, but unfortunately, he couldn't actually call the man that. He also *had* to answer because Asshat would kick his ass if he didn't. He'd probably make a point of visiting the coven just to do it.

"Maurice! What can I do for you?" Fyfe said, hoping to shock Asshat with how happy he sounded. Or at least he hoped he sounded happy, as opposed to annoyed and ready to hang up at any second.

"What the fuck do you think you're doing, Fyfe?" Maurice's voice boomed.

Fyfe grimaced. "Answering my phone?"

"Stop playing the idiot. You know what I'm talking about."

Fyfe knew. How could he not? He leaned back in his chair and looked at the ceiling. "He encroached on my territory. He didn't tell me he was in town. He attacked a friend."

"A friend, but not a coven member."

Fyfe sighed. He knew he should have insisted that Percy become a coven member, but Percy had said no, and Fyfe valued their friendship too much to push. "That doesn't mean I shouldn't protect him. Besides, Vlad attacked and bit a human. You know the punishment for that."

Maurice snorted. "Of course I do. I wrote the damn law. You should have called us, though, instead of meting your own justice."

"I couldn't exactly ask him to wait until your guys got here. Come on, Maurice. No one is going to care. Vlad was nuts. He kept another vampire in chains for years. He came after him once he managed to escape. I should have called the conclave, but we both know you guys would have killed him."

Maurice sighed. "Yes, they would have. And I don't care. But not every conclave member feels the way I do. You shouldn't take advantage of the soft spot I have for you."

Fyfe grinned. "Soft spot, huh?" Maybe he *should* have called Maurice by the nickname he had for him.

"Don't be an asshole."

"Why did you call? Is it only to berate me, or did you have something else to tell me?"

"Some of the conclave members aren't happy, Fyfe. They wanted to make you pay for what happened."

Fyfe snorted. "As if they would have done anything differently."

"Be that as it may. They're the ones questioning your actions right now, not the opposite. And they're in the conclave, so they are the ones with the power. You need to be careful."

"You know that's never been my forte."

"It's not, but you have to toe the line right now before they find a reason to take the coven away from you."

That was Fyfe's worst fear. He might have never wanted or expected to take over the coven, but he had, and they were his to protect. He swallowed and tried to find a way to tell Maurice he'd behave without actually giving in. "I'll protect the coven," was the only thing he could come up with.

Maurice's voice was softer when he answered. "I know. You take your role seriously. I just wanted to warn you."

Since the conclave had the power to get rid of him and put someone else in charge of the coven, Fyfe was glad for the warning. "Thanks."

"And, Fyfe?"

"Yes?"

"I'm not sure of anything, but I think one of the conclave members has someone inside."

It took Fyfe's brain a second to understand what that meant. "You mean in the coven?"

"Yes. I was given a lot of details about what happened with Vlad. Too many details, if you know what I mean. So be careful, and think about cleaning your act up, yeah?"

"Of course." Who could it be? Fyfe had always known not every member was happy with the way he led the coven. He hadn't expected them to be. Everyone had their own opinions, including him, and since he was the coven leader, he was the only one making decisions. Some of the elders didn't like that. They probably would have snatched the spot as coven leader if they'd been able to, but Fyfe had been the one who'd killed the old leader, so the coven was legally his, not theirs.

Never theirs, because Fyfe knew what would happen if he allowed that. "I'll keep my eyes open."

"Good. And let me know if you need anything. And I mean *anything*, Fyfe. We might not see eye to eye all the time, but you're doing a good job as that coven's leader. I want that to continue. It's one less coven I have to worry about."

Fyfe couldn't help but smile. "Ah, so you do love me."

"I wouldn't call it that."

Maurice hung up without adding anything. Fyfe was still

grinning when he hung up, but that didn't last long, not when he heard the yells in the hallway.

He pushed up from his chair and stomped to the door. The coven knew better than to fight, especially where Fyfe could hear them. He didn't care about fighting as long as he didn't find out about it and it wasn't serious. Some people might think vampires were dead and cold, but when it came to emotions and feelings, nothing could be further from the truth. Being immortal meant they had plenty of time to let things steep until they exploded.

Just like it seemed to have happened in the hallway outside his office.

Andrew and Falkner were hitting each other at the top of the stairs. They didn't even notice Fyfe, not until he grabbed Andrew and pulled him back, Falkner's fist hitting his face instead of Andrew's.

The three of them froze.

Fyfe swore and rubbed his cheek. "What the fuck are the two of you doing?" he snapped.

Andrew looked sheepish. "Sorry. It's nothing."

"Nothing? You two were punching each other outside of my office door. You *know* I don't want anyone fighting in the house."

"We weren't really fighting."

"My face says otherwise."

Falkner winced. "I'm sorry. But we weren't fighting."

Fyfe sighed. He didn't want to have to police his coven members like a father. He *wasn't* their father, and just the thought made him shudder in horror, especially when he thought about the elder members. Some of them were twice his age. "I don't care what's going on between the two of you, but take it somewhere else."

Falkner nodded so hard, Fyfe wondered if his head might fall off and bounce down the stairs. "We're going."

"You do that." Fyfe watched them leave. He tried to look at them critically and see if they'd only been playing around. They weren't shying from each other. In fact, they leaned close enough to whisper like children, so Fyfe was pretty sure Andrew had told him the truth. Whatever it was they'd been fighting over, it wasn't serious.

At least this had been an easy problem to solve. Fyfe's conclave problem wouldn't be solved as smoothly, and Fyfe knew he had to get ready for a fight—a real one this time. He sighed and rubbed his face. It didn't actually hurt, although it had when Falkner had punched him. It gave him an excuse to stop working, though, at least for the rest of the night. Dawn would happen in a few hours, so he still had time to go out for a walk. It was his favorite time of the day—when the streets were empty, and no one thought it weird to find him walking around the city. If he stuck to the worst part of the city, it was guaranteed no one would bother him. It wasn't like he wouldn't be safe, even if some bad people were around. He'd make dog kibble out of them and feed them to the nearest werewolf pack.

Fyfe snuck out of the mansion, praying no one would see him. He knew they'd stop him if they did. There was always at least one problem for him to solve with the coven, and he wasn't up for that right now. He wasn't up for dealing with the coven in any way, shape, or form right now.

He took a deep breath, inhaling the night air. He already felt better. The walls weren't closing in around him anymore. Sometimes he wished he could leave, abandon the coven he'd never meant to lead, and travel like he'd done for so long. He missed it. He missed being alone, not having anyone depending on him.

But he couldn't change it.

James curled onto himself to avoid the blows. He didn't know where they came from, and his werewolf wasn't happy about still being chained to the fucking sink. It meant he couldn't defend them, but that was okay. James didn't mind being beaten up. Maybe he'd even die, and he wouldn't have to keep on running.

A kick landed against his stomach, pain exploding. He needed to curl himself tighter, but he wasn't sure he could.

Then the kicks stopped. James' werewolf wanted him to get up and fight, but he screwed his eyes shut and waited. He wasn't sure what for—more kicks? The bite of a weapon in his flesh?

None of that came.

The moon had started to wane. Its pull was weaker, and it allowed James to start thinking again. He wasn't free enough to shift back yet, but at least he was aware of his surroundings. It wouldn't help him much if he needed to defend himself. He was weak because of the shift that was coming, and he'd been beaten up. But he was aware enough to know there were only two heartbeats in the room now.

He opened his eyes and noticed the vampire watching him right away. He didn't know how long the guy had been there, why he'd killed the man beating James and had decided to hang around, but he seemed comfortable. He was leaning his shoulder against the wall, and his arms crossed over his chest. His dark hair was braided and fell over his shoulder. He was wearing a long black coat and black jeans. James couldn't see what color his eyes were, but he was gorgeous, and James wasn't wearing clothes, which meant the vampire would notice it right away if he got hard.

That was, if he didn't kill James first.

The vampire pushed away from the wall and came to crouch next to James. James held his breath, sure that these were the last moments of his life. He could defend himself, of course, but he was still chained to the wall, and he was a young werewolf. He didn't know the vampire, but he could tell he was an old one. He'd be fast and strong, and he'd kill James easily.

Maybe it wouldn't be that bad. It was what the conclave was going to do to James anyway if they caught him, and he was tired of running. He wanted to settle down, get a house and live his life. He'd never have that, though, not with the conclave nipping at his heels.

Death sounded kind of appealing right now.

The vampire reached for James, and James closed his eyes. He might not care about dying, but that didn't mean he wanted to see it coming.

But instead of hands wrapping around his head to snap his neck or the cold feeling of a blade against his throat, James felt . . . a finger poking at his cheek?

He opened his eyes. The vampire was leaning over him, and he *was* poking him with a finger as if he didn't know James could bite it off if he wanted to. It would be easy, considering how close it was to his mouth.

"You know, chaining yourself to the wall isn't the best way to deal with your furry half," the vampire said.

James resisted the urge to roll his eyes. As if he didn't know that. He knew he needed to learn how to deal with his werewolf half, but how was he supposed to do that? No one would help him do it, and he couldn't exactly pull a how-to book out of his ass, or even find one in the closest bookstore. No, the only way to learn control over his werewolf was to have someone who knew teach him, and since he was being hunted, he didn't have a line of volunteers waiting for the chance to do it.

"You would have been able to kill that man if you'd been free from that chain," the vampire said.

This time, James *did* roll his eyes. It made the vampire

chuckle. James wasn't sure why the man wasn't killing him. It was well-known that vampires and werewolves hated each other, which was why this situation didn't make sense. James needed to talk to this guy, dammit. He couldn't, not until his mouth shifted back to human. He hadn't yet mastered talking with the werewolf's huge ass fangs.

The vampire chuckled. "Okay. You're not going to attack me if I free you, are you? Because I'm sorry to say this, but I'll beat you if you do."

James shook his head. He'd never hurt anyone in his human form—or in his werewolf form if he had anything to say about it. He'd been lucky enough to find a pack almost right after he'd been turned, and while he hadn't managed to learn control yet, the pack had helped to make sure he stayed safe, at least until they'd accused him of killing the alpha and had tried to hand him over to the conclave.

But even though he hadn't shifted back yet, he was in control.

The vampire smiled. "Good. Stay still. Those handcuffs did a number on your wrist, you know. You shouldn't use them."

James grunted. The vampire's touch was light as he ran his fingers over the cuffs and found the lock. James nodded toward the sink, and the vampire looked up. James had left the keys on it, and the vampire reached for it, uncuffing James and letting the handcuffs and the chains fall to the floor. They jingled and clanged, and James felt lighter. He stretched, making sure he didn't touch the vampire, and raised his arm to examine his wrist. It was red, the skin raw and peeling in some places under the receding hair, but he'd heal fast. It was one of the perks of being a werewolf.

He sat up and leaned against the wall. He felt weak and like he could eat a horse. He wasn't ready to get up yet, but he folded his knees to hide his groin. He hated feeling this vulnerable, especially when he was with someone he didn't know. How was he supposed to trust this guy? He might have already called the conclave. He didn't have a reason to, but he might have. Or he could be planning to kill James. Even though James was a werewolf, he was weak right now. He wouldn't be able to do much to defend himself.

The vampire stood over him, looking down, and that didn't help James feel better. He could feel himself shifting back to human, though, and he was glad that when he tried to talk, his human voice came out rather than grunts. It was still rough and borderline animalistic, but it was understandable. "Are you going to kill me?"

The vampire's eyes widened. "God, no. Why would I do that?"

"Because you're a vampire."

"And you're a werewolf. I'm aware of that."

"We should hate each other."

"I supposed we should. It's what everyone thinks, isn't it?"

"Yes." It was what he'd been taught when he'd become a werewolf.

The vampire tsked. "You'll find out that what everyone thinks doesn't always matter, pup."

James narrowed his eyes. "Don't call me that."

"Why not? You're just a pup, aren't you? How long have you been a werewolf?"

"Six months."

"See? A pup."

James glared. "I don't like you."

The vampire grinned. "But it's not because I'm a vampire."

"No. it's because you're annoying."

"I was right, then."

James rubbed his face. "What do you want from me?"

"Well, a thank you for saving your life wouldn't be bad, since I *did* save your life."

James looked around. The body was slumped in the corner, his face toward the wall, so James couldn't see it. He didn't think he *wanted* to see. He was sorry the guy was dead, but it had been him or James, and James liked being alive most of the time, or he had before, anyway. "Thank you," he croaked.

"Why did he attack you?"

"I don't know. I spent the night here to be sure I wouldn't hurt anyone. I'm not even sure how he found me."

"What are you doing here, pup?"

James knew glaring wouldn't help with the nickname. "I was staying out of the way until I was sure I wasn't dangerous anymore. What are *you* doing here?"

"Taking a walk. Saving your life, apparently. I'm Fyfe."

James swallowed. He shouldn't tell Fyfe who he was, but he was tired of running and being alone. "James."

"Ah, like my king."

"What?"

Fyfe waved. "Never mind. Are you feeling up to getting dressed? I'd like to be home before the sun comes up. I know it doesn't bother you, but it *does* bother me."

James blinked. "What do you mean, home before the sun comes up?"

Fyfe wasn't sure what to do with the werewolf — with James. He was the last thing Fyfe had expected to encounter on his walk. He came to this part of town often, yet he'd only ever crossed paths with homeless people and feral cats. He certainly had never needed to kill anyone. Beat up, yes, when they'd tried to steal his wallet once, but not kill.

Not that he cared about the body on the other side of the

room. The man had been attacking James, and Fyfe didn't regret killing him. He didn't care that James was a werewolf. He'd been honest when he'd told James that not all vampires hated werewolves. He thought it was ridiculous. Werewolves had never done anything to him, so why should he hate them? They were just people, like him, and they just wanted to live their lives without having to fight bloodsuckers.

He was all for that.

James staggered to his feet, and Fyfe reached out by instinct, wrapping his hand around James' arm and holding him upright. "Are you okay?" he asked. He already knew the answer to that. It was obvious James had no control over his wolf form, and that meant that the shifts were brutal instead of smooth like they were supposed to be. He also seemed to be underfed and looked like he hadn't slept well in a while, which didn't help.

James shrugged. And almost fell on his ass. "I've been better, but what do you care?"

"I'm not going to leave you here when you can't even defend yourself."

The fur was receding from James' body, and the fangs in his mouth had gone back to their normal human size. His hair was actually hair now rather than fur, and Fyfe wanted to card his fingers through it because it was a gorgeous mass of light brown and blond. It was too long and what Fyfe would call shaggy, but it suited James. Fyfe had always thought werewolves looked awkward in their shifted form, not quite human and not quite animal, a mix of the two, but James' human body was beautiful.

Fyfe stopped resisting and pulled on a strand of James' hair. "You've been on the streets for a while, haven't you?" he murmured.

James' back went rigid, and he stepped away—and

promptly stumbled.

Fyfe grabbed him and pulled him close. "I'm sorry. I didn't want to offend you. I just don't like this."

James tried to push away, but he wasn't putting much energy into it. He needed food and rest, especially after the shift. "You think *I* like it?" he snapped. He sighed and leaned against Fyfe's chest, and the little thrill of victory in Fyfe's chest shifted to something warm when he looked up. "I don't have a choice."

"Where's your pack, pup?"

James looked away. "I don't have one, not anymore."

There was a story there, and Fyfe would get it eventually. Not now, though. The sun was coming up, and he needed to be home before that happened if he didn't want to be covered in rashes and blisters.

Fyfe had a choice. He needed to leave, and he needed to do it as soon as possible. He could leave James here and forget about him, or he could take him with him and sneak him into the mansion and take care of him. He knew which one he wanted to do. It was stupid and reckless, especially after the call with Maurice, but Fyfe liked to listen to his instincts, and they were telling him James wasn't dangerous, not to him anyway. He was a werewolf, so he wasn't innocuous either, but Fyfe didn't think he was a bad man or that he'd attack him or the coven.

There was only one way to ascertain that.

Fyfe looked down and brushed a strand of hair away from James' face. "You need to get dressed."

James rolled his eyes. "I know I do." He cleared his throat. His cheeks flushed, and he looked everywhere but at Fyfe. "Thanks for helping me. I don't know what would have happened if you hadn't, but I can imagine. I'll be more careful in the future." He pushed away from Fyfe, and this time, Fyfe let him go. He hovered close, but James stayed on his feet. "You should probably go," he told Fyfe. "I know the sun is coming up."

This was it. "Come with me."

James blinked. He was still out of it, still shifting to his human form. The fur was almost gone, though, and it had left place to pale, soft-looking skin Fyfe wanted to touch.

He needed to stop thinking with his dick.

He leaned down to grab the clothes that poked out of the backpack by the wall. "Come on. The sooner we leave, the better I'll feel."

"And you want me to go with you?"

"Yes."

"*Why?*"

"Why not?"

James accepted the clothes Fyfe was holding out. "Why? How about because you don't know me? Or because I'm a werewolf and you're a vampire? Or maybe there's no way your coven leader will accept me anywhere near the coven."

Fyfe grinned. "Oh, he will."

James put his t-shirt on. "You sound sure of that."

"That's because I am. I happen to be my coven's leader, and I say you're welcome."

James frowned. He reached down to push his legs into his jeans, and Fyfe looked away. He was *not* going to ogle James' ass, not right now. Later, though, he definitely was going to, once James wasn't as vulnerable. "What about your coven members? There's no way they'll accept that."

"Good thing they'll have to if they don't want me to kick their asses, then."

"You're not that kind of leader."

Fyfe arched a brow. "How do you know that?" James was right, of course, but Fyfe didn't understand how he could look so convinced of it.

James shrugged. "I don't know. I don't think you'd have

helped me if you were a bad man. You could have walked past the warehouse. You could have ignored the guy beating me up. You could have left as soon as you killed him. You didn't have to stay and make sure I was okay, especially considering everything."

"Everything?"

James gestured between the two of them. "You know. The werewolf-vampire thing, or even the fact that you don't know me. I could be a serial killer as far as you know."

Fyfe snorted. "A serial killer? Yeah, right. You look as menacing and threatening as my grandmother."

"She's still alive?"

"Fuck no. I was born in sixteen-seventeen. She died a while ago. That doesn't change the fact that you look like you couldn't hurt a fly even if you tried."

James crossed his arms over his chest and glared. "I'm a werewolf."

"I'm aware of that." Fyfe tapped the side of his nose. "I can smell it, and of course, the fact that you were all furry when I came in is also a *big* indication."

"You're a vampire."

Fyfe sighed and pinched the bridge of his nose. "Again, I'm aware of that. I haven't been human in a while. Look, you can say no." Fyfe hoped he wouldn't, though. He wasn't sure what it was about James, but he wanted to get to know him. He wanted to be more than just the coven leader for once. He knew his friends and the people in the coven loved and respected him, but he wanted more. He wanted true love. It had been too long since he'd last had that.

He wasn't sure why he thought he could have it with James. It was ridiculous. They didn't know each other. But he'd been lucky enough to have people help him when he'd needed it. He wanted to do the same for James. He so obviously needed it. He shouldn't be living on the streets and hiding out in abandoned warehouses. He shouldn't be alone when he shifted during the full moon. Fyfe could tell there was more to James' situation than James had told him, but he wasn't worried. Just like James knew Fyfe wouldn't hurt him, Fyfe knew James was safe. He wasn't dangerous. Whatever had happened to him, whatever had made him leave his pack, he wasn't at fault.

Fyfe cleared his throat. "Look, you can stay here, or you can come with me, but if you're coming, we have to go. The sun's coming up, and I don't want to end up with blisters. I can promise you, you'll be safe with the coven. Not every member will be happy when they find out about you, but again, I'm the leader. What I say goes. What do *you* say?"

Chapter Two

At first, James wasn't sure where he was when he opened his eyes. Even when he'd lived at home, or later with the pack, his bedroom hadn't been like this. He was used to cheap furniture and bedding, not *this*.

The ceiling was dark and rimmed with thick wooden beams. In contrast, the walls were a light blue, while the furniture—including the bed he was in—was the same dark wood color of the beams. And the sheets. James didn't think he'd ever felt anything as soft as the sheets on this bed.

There was a door in front of the bed. It was open enough that James could see it was the bathroom. The windows on his left were covered with curtains, not one inch of them letting the outside light pass—if there was light outside. He had no idea what time it was, but considering he was in a vampire coven, it was probably night.

The fireplace in the corner on his right held a crackling fire that made James feel warm and secure. He wasn't sure he had a reason to feel that way. As far as he knew, he was in the enemy's den. Why had he accepted to come this morning? Why had he thought it was a good idea?

He pressed the back of his head against the pillow. He wasn't sure what had happened last night—or rather, morning. He remembered coming home with Fyfe, and Fyfe putting him into bed, but that was about it. He was always a little out of it after the full moon, and the fact that he hadn't been eating or sleeping well in the past month wasn't helping. He'd been out to the world until now, and he didn't know where Fyfe was.

What if he'd left and someone found him? James had a hard time believing the other vampires wouldn't have a problem with him being there. Did they even know about him? They'd no doubt eventually smell him. There was no way he could hide his werewolf scent, especially not to vampires.

The door creaked open. James panicked and slid off the bed on the side of the windows—the side opposite the door. He took the blanket with him even though he knew hiding under them wouldn't help. The bed smelled of Fyfe, though, so maybe the person coming in would think it was him.

And fuck, had Fyfe really put James in his bed? Where had he slept today, then?

"It's only me," Fyfe said.

James relaxed. He pulled the blanket off his face and peeked above the bed. Fyfe walked in, holding a tray. He kicked the door shut and locked it after putting the tray down on the dresser next to the door. "What are you doing on the floor?"

"I didn't know it was you. What is this place? Is it your bedroom?"

"Of course it is. I couldn't very well give you a guest room, not when no one knows you're here."

"They don't know?"

"Not yet. I'll tell them. Eventually."

James groaned. "I can't stay if no one wants me here."

"Who said no one wanted you? I do. I wouldn't have given you my room if I didn't."

"Where did you sleep?"

Fyfe grinned. His fangs gleamed in the light from the fireplace. "In my bed, of course."

"But . . . *I* was in your bed."

"It's a big bed."

James gaped. "You mean you slept with me?"

"I didn't touch you inappropriately, don't worry. We just slept. I like my men to be awake when I have sex with them. It's more fun that way."

James closed his mouth with a snap and looked down at himself. He was still mostly dressed. He was wearing the t-shirt he'd put on last night—that morning, damn it. He also had his jeans on, but his feet were bare, so Fyfe had at least taken off his shoes. Nothing else, though.

"I'd have taken your jeans off, but I know you're not wearing anything under them. I don't know about you, but I *hate* sleeping in jeans. They're uncomfortable," Fyfe said.

He was wearing pajama pants that looked soft, and a t-shirt. It was far from the way he'd looked last night, sophisticated and handsome. He was still gorgeous, but he looked comfortable and intimate, like Sunday mornings and nights spent in bed talking.

James swallowed. "I've been sleeping in them for weeks."

Fyfe grimaced. "That's what I thought. I brought you food, and if you give me your clothes, I'll wash them. You can shower, and if you don't have clean clothes, I can lend you some. You're bulkier than me and shorter, but I'm sure some of my stuff will fit you."

"I should go." James got up and bundled the blanket, dropping it at the foot of the bed. He walked around it, but Fyfe snatched his wrist and tugged. His hand was warm and soft. James wasn't sure what he'd expected, but werewolves never talked of vampires except to curse them and berate them. He had no idea what vampires really were like. He'd been told they were monsters, cold-blooded killers.

But Fyfe wasn't. He was warm, and he'd taken care of James last night, this morning, even though they didn't know each other. He hadn't had to. He could easily have left the warehouse and James behind. He should have. Even though he was the coven leader, it didn't mean he wouldn't end up in trouble for this.

Yet here they were.

"Don't go. You're safe here," Fyfe murmured.

James wanted to believe him. He hadn't felt safe in months. Even when he'd been with the pack, he hadn't felt safe—and he'd been right to feel that way. The pack had used him as a scapegoat. They'd killed the alpha, the only person who'd agreed to help James, and had cast the blame on him. Would Fyfe believe him if he told him that, though? Or would he call the conclave and have him arrested? James wanted to trust him, but could he?

"When the rest of the coven finds out about me . . ."

Fyfe let go of James' wrist.

James wanted his touch again. He didn't dare ask for it, though. They weren't friends. They didn't know each other.

"They'll have to accept you." Fyfe's voice was hard now.

He really believed what he was saying, and James wanted to, too. He couldn't, though. Even if he did have a place with the coven, and he didn't, he needed to leave. The conclave would eventually find him, and he couldn't drag Fyfe and his coven down with him. "I'm going to have to go sooner or later."

Fyfe cocked his head. "What are you hiding from, James?"

James shook his head. He wasn't going to tell Fyfe. He didn't want Fyfe to look at him with horror like the pack members who hadn't been in on the cover-up had. He didn't want him to think he was a monster, a murderer. "I can't stay. I'm grateful for what you did for me. I'm not sure why you did it, but thank you. I can't abuse your hospitality."

Fyfe sighed. "Why don't you eat while the food is still warm? You can shower when you're done, and I'll make sure you have clean clothes. We can talk after that."

"There's nothing to say."

"Oh, yes, there is. I know we don't know each other, James, but I'm not a quitter, especially not when I take on projects."

"I'm not a project."

"You're right, you're not. But you're a person, someone I'd like to get to know better."

James hated that he wanted the same thing, and even more that he couldn't have it. "I don't." He didn't want to hurt Fyfe, but maybe it was for the best. He'd get over whatever he was doing easily enough.

Fyfe snorted. "That's not going to work, pup. Now eat. We don't have food in the house, so I got you fast food. I had it delivered."

James couldn't help but look at the tray. He hadn't noticed it before, but there was a burger and fries, and the smell made his stomach growl. He swallowed. "Look, I thank you for everything, the bed, and the food, but I'm going to have to leave once I'm done eating."

"You keep thinking that, pup. We'll talk about it later, though."

Fyfe got the wet clothes out of the washing machine and pushed them into the dryer. He hummed as he worked, his thoughts never far from James. He wanted to help, but he couldn't unless James let him in.

Fyfe grinned at himself. He wanted James to let him in in more ways than just telling him what was going on, but he could wait and give him time. That was, if he stayed with the coven. And if he stayed, Fyfe was going to have to find a way to get the coven to accept him.

He probably wouldn't have too many problems with the younger members. The coven had a reputation for accepting rogue vamps, vamps who'd been cast out of their own covens or hadn't been able to find one, to begin with. Some of them had been bitten and turned by accident. Some had had to face turning into vampires alone, and they'd had trouble with it.

Fyfe didn't care about the past. As long as they behaved themselves now that they were part of his coven, he wasn't going to kick them out. He didn't care how many people they'd killed, or that they were gay, or even that they were in love with humans or other supernatural creatures. He'd been trying to open up the coven, but between the vampire conclave members and the older members of the coven, he hadn't had much success. It would take a much bigger change for people to let him do what he wanted with his coven. The conclave would no doubt try to get him kicked out as the leader if he allowed other supernatural creatures in, and that went especially for werewolves. Vampires and wolves didn't have the best past. It was stupid and ridiculous, but it was what it was, and Fyfe was only a man. He couldn't' change the world.

"You sound happy," a voice said.

Fyfe hoped the way he'd startled wasn't obvious. He smiled up at Archie as he straightened. "You need to do laundry?"

"I was actually wondering why *you* were doing laundry."

"Uh, because I need clean clothes?"

"Except you washed your clothes yesterday."

"I spilled stuff. And it's not your business."

Archie shrugged. "Sorry I asked. I didn't mean to be pushy."

Fyfe liked Archie. He'd been kicked out of his first coven sixty years ago when the leader had found him with his then human boyfriend. He'd been on his own for decades, and Fyfe had saved him from being torn apart by a group of werewolves.

Fyfe bit his lower lip. Would that fact mean that Archie was going to be against James staying with them? Archie had always been on Fyfe's side. He'd trusted Fyfe to make the best decisions for the coven. Would that still be true once he found out about James? Or would he let prejudice tinge his view of James and his actions? "What do you think or werewolves?" Fyfe blurted out.

Archie blinked. "Werewolves?"

"Yes."

"I hate them."

Fyfe felt like he might throw up the blood he'd had for breakfast. "Because of what they did to you?"

"Of course. You know what happened and how close I was to dying. Why are you even asking me that?"

"Never mind. I'm going back to my room. Don't touch my laundry, even if it's done. I'll be back later to get the clothes."

"Fyfe, wait."

"I don't have time right now."

Fyfe sighed. That could have gone better. He'd hoped Archie would be on his side, but apparently, he wouldn't. Fyfe wasn't sure what it would mean yet, but he was going to find out, because James wasn't going anywhere, not if Fyfe had something to say about it—and he did.

James was still in the bathroom when Fyfe got back to the bedroom. He'd been in there for what had to be close to an hour, but from what he'd said, Fyfe knew it had been a while since he'd been safe, sated, and able to shower. He could stay in there for as long as he wanted to. Fyfe was going to have to go to his office soon, though. Someone was bound to need something, and they'd look for him here if he wasn't in the office. Sometimes he still wondered why he hadn't let the conclave pick another leader for the coven.

He'd never meant to be a coven leader or any kind of leader. He still didn't think it was a good idea. He was him, and that meant he couldn't be a good leader. But he'd done his best until now. Surely no one would blame him for wanting something or someone for himself, right?

He knew better than to believe that, though.

He was glad when James came out of the bathroom, his hair still dark with water and curling around his face, his cheeks flushed. He was wearing a pair of Fyfe's sweatpants and one of his t-shirts, and he looked lickable. Fyfe wanted to taste him, so he stayed far away, just in case his hands and his mouth decided to move on their own. "Feel better?"

James nodded. "Yeah, thanks. I can't remember the last time a shower felt this good. Even when I was with the pack—"

Fyfe desperately wanted him to continue, but he let it go—for now. "Your clothes are in the dryer, so I should have them back to you soon. In the meantime, you should probably stay here. Not that I want you to feel like a prisoner, but the coven doesn't know about you yet, so I need to talk to them before they find out. Things are always worse when they're surprised."

"Fyfe—"

"Nope. I know what you're going to say, and I don't want to hear it. I won't force you to stay, of course, but you should take a few days, even if you want to leave. You can rest and eat, and don't think about whatever problems are weighing on your shoulders. They'll no doubt still be there once you go."

But the thing was that Fyfe didn't want him to go. It had been a while since he'd been this interested in someone, probably close to seventy years. It didn't happen often, and he didn't want to give it up. He knew it was selfish, but with his life being infinitely long, he wanted to grab that kind of connection every time it happened. He wouldn't let go of James without a fight, even if the person he'd have to fight was James.

He sat on the edge of the mattress. "You're obviously running from something or someone."

James nodded curtly. "You're right, I am."

Fyfe hated that he'd been right, at least this time. "Is it dangerous for the coven? I need to know at least that. I'm their leader, and that means I'm their safety net. I need to protect them." They came before James, and even before Fyfe. That was something Fyfe had had to learn over the years. He might not like it, but he had a responsibility toward them, and he was going to uphold it.

James paled. "I . . ."

"I won't kick you out. You don't even have to tell me who's after you or why, although I'd appreciate those details. But I need to keep everyone safe, including you."

"I'm not one of your coven members."

"You're right, you're not, but I saved your life yesterday, and I don't want that to be wasted. I brought you into my home and let you sleep in my bed. I bought you food. All those things might not mean much to you modern people, but it does for me. Of course, I was born in a different time, so I understand we have different upbringings. But you're under my protection as much as everyone else in this house. Now." Fyfe realized that was dangerous, but he wasn't going to change it. He'd given James his word, and it meant something to him. It meant *everything*.

"I should tell you everything," James said. It was obvious he didn't want to.

"Probably."

"I'm afraid . . . I'm afraid you'll kick me out if I do. I know it would be for the best, but I don't want to get back out there."

"I understand."

James shook his head. "No, you don't."

"James, I've had people hunting me. Four hundred years is a long time to be alive. I've made my share of enemies."

James looked straight at Fyfe. "But was any of those enemies the conclave?"

James shouldn't have said that, but he understood where Fyfe was coming from. He was the coven leader, and that meant that he led them, but also that he protected them to the best of his ability. Taking in a werewolf who was being hunted by the conclave wasn't the best way to do that. James was glad he'd had a day to rest, eat, and wash, but he'd always known it wouldn't last much more than that. He couldn't put Fyfe and his coven in danger, not after Fyfe had been so good to him. Besides, there was no way Fyfe would still want him around once he found out why the conclave was after him.

Fyfe blinked. "The conclave."

Dammit. James didn't want to do this. Fyfe had been so nice to him. He didn't want to see horror and fear in his eyes—and he didn't want to get beat up within an inch of his life like he had yesterday. He was still aching and sore, and while shifting back to his human form had helped, it hadn't worked a miracle. James could defend himself, but against a vampire that was as old and experienced as Fyfe, he didn't stand a chance. "Yes."

Fyfe frowned. "You're telling me that the reason you were hiding in the warehouse yesterday, the reason you chained yourself to a fucking wall, is because you're running from the conclave?"

James swallowed. "Yes." He cleared his throat. "I should probably go now. I know you won't want me around since you know, and well, the sooner I leave town, the better it will be for me. I'd ask you not to contact the conclave, but I know it's your duty, so—"

"Sit the fuck down."

James' eyes widened. "What?"

Fyfe pointed at his bed. "Park your ass there and don't move."

James had never been beaten up on a bed. Maybe the softness would help.

Fyfe walked back and forth in front of the bed. He was still frowning. He was also muttering to himself, and James thought he heard the word *asshat*, but he wasn't sure. He didn't want to interrupt Fyfe since it didn't look like he was going to beat him up right now, and that was a win in James' book.

Fyfe stopped in front of James. "Tell me."

"Tell you what?"

Fyfe rolled his eyes. "What happened, James. Why is the conclave after you? What do they think you've done?"

"*Think* I've done? Why do you think I haven't done what they accused me of?"

"I've been dealing with the conclave for hundreds of years. I know them. There are good people there, of course, but there are also bad ones and lazy ones. A lot of them are content with accepting what's being told because it's easier. So, what happened? Why are they after you?"

James rubbed his face. He didn't want to have to go through this again, but the fact that Fyfe hadn't kicked him out yet made him hope. He was lonely. He didn't have anyone, and while he barely knew Fyfe, he'd already been there for him more than most people in his life. He wasn't stepping back, either. No, he seemed to want to face James' problems and maybe even try to solve them, and for the first time in a long time, James found himself hoping.

"I was bitten about a year ago. I don't remember much of the first six months. You saw I can't control my shifts or my werewolf form yet. I spent the first six or so months alone because I was terrified of what I was and that I would hurt people. I left my life behind. I didn't even know for sure *what* I was until I found the pack." James licked his lips. "They took me in. They didn't have to, and I'm grateful that they did. The alpha made that decision, of course. Not everyone was happy with it, but then, they weren't happy with him most of the time."

James didn't want to go on. He hated thinking back to that time. Alpha Torres had taken him in even when he hadn't had to. It hadn't been home, but it had been better than the loneliness of the woods.

"What happened, James?" Fyfe asked, his voice soft.

James didn't look at him. "I did my best to learn control and to blend in, but I was always the outsider, so it was easy for the beta and his cronies to blame it on me when they killed Alpha Torres."

Fyfe swore. "That's why the conclave wants you?"

"Yes. Alpha Torres was killed, and his beta took his place right away. Then he threw me into a cell and called the conclave, telling them I'd gone crazy and that I'd killed Alpha Torres. They didn't even investigate when they got there. They just decided that the beta had to be right. They were going to execute me."

Fyfe snorted. "I'm not surprised. That's their go-to solution. What happened? How did you escape? The conclave enforcers aren't known to let people go by accident. They might be unthinking brutes, but they know how to do their jobs."

"I had help. I'd made a friend while I was with the pack. Oscar. He's the beta's son, and he's been a werewolf since birth. I think he had a crush on me. Anyway, he was my only real friend there, and he risked a lot by sneaking me out at night. I wanted him to come with me, but—" James shrugged. "The pack is his family."

"And the conclave is still after you?"

"Yeah. I've never been able to put more than a few days between us, and trust me, I've tried. They always manage to find me."

"That's because they know what you're going to do. They talked with the beta and other people who know you, so they're aware of the fact that you don't know anyone else in the supernatural community. That means you'll stick with what you know. In your case, it's empty warehouses and dingy motels. It's easy enough to find you that way." Fyfe grinned. "But of course, they didn't think you might make friends while you were on the run."

"Friends?"

Fyfe rolled his eyes. "You know what I mean."

James thought so, but he didn't understand it. "Why would you want to help me? The conclave can cause you a lot of problems if they find out you've been helping me, and I know the coven is important to you."

"Of course it's important to me. I'm the leader. That doesn't mean I'm going to look the other way when the conclave and their goons are behaving like assholes."

"The enforcers are doing their jobs." James didn't fully understand how the conclave worked—no one had taken the time to explain it to him. Hell, he hadn't even known the conclave existed until the enforcers had arrived and told him they were going to kill him for murdering Alpha Torres. But he could work it out, and it wasn't good for him.

"The enforcers are idiots who couldn't tell their feet from their asses even if they had a map explaining it."

James chuckled. It had been a while since he'd laughed, and since he'd felt safe. He knew it was only an illusion and that it would only last for the time he stayed with Fyfe, but it was more than he'd expected and let himself hope for. Being with Fyfe was a reprieve, but James didn't fool himself. No matter what Fyfe thought or was saying, the best outcome of this would be for James to leave before the conclave was made aware of his presence in the house where the coven lived.

"I can't ask you to go against the conclave for me." James got up. He liked it here too much, so the sooner he got out, the better and the easier it would be, for him and everyone involved.

Fyfe pushed James back on the bed. "Stay."

James glared. "I'm not a dog."

"But you do get furry once a month."

"Should I call you bloodsucker, then?"

Fyfe's grin widened. "Why not? It is what I am after all. I've never understood why so many vampires take it as an insult." His smile faded. "Stay here, please. Don't leave yet. I told you there are a few good people in the conclave, and I want to reach out to them. I won't tell them you're here, but I *will* ask you be given an investigation, at the very least."

"They're going to realize what it means. That I'm here."

"Probably. But they're friends, so they won't send the enforcers here."

James wanted to believe Fyfe. He wasn't sure he could, but he sat back down anyway.

Fyfe couldn't stop thinking about what had happened to James as he walked to his office. He wasn't surprised by what he'd learned, and he didn't doubt James had told him the truth. It wasn't the first time something like that happened, and it wouldn't be the last one, either. Fyfe couldn't help all the people unjustly accused and killed by the conclave and their enforcers, but he *could* help James. He wanted to, as stupid as it probably was.

So Fyfe called Maurice.

"Please tell me you didn't kill someone else," Maurice grumbled when he answered.

"Not yet."

"Yet, Fyfe? Did you hear what I told you before, or were you playing tic tac toe while I was speaking?"

"I wouldn't be playing tic tac toe. I *might* play with myself, but you're not my first choice for phone sex." No, that first choice was in Fyfe's room right now, showering.

Maurice groaned. "What do you need now?"

Fyfe leaned back in his chair. He needed to find a way to have Maurice investigate without him suspecting he was hiding James. They were friends, even though Maurice was an asshole most of the time, and Fyfe trusted him, but would Maurice put Fyfe above his duty to the conclave? "I need help."

"Of course you do. Talk."

"I have . . . a friend."

"I don't want to know anything about your sex life, Fyfe."

"Not that kind of friend." Not yet anyway, although Fyfe hadn't given up on having it with James. He just needed to make sure James felt safe and knew he had a choice first. The last thing he wanted was for James to think that having sex with him was necessary for him to stay with the coven.

"I find it hard to believe but go on."

"He's in trouble. The conclave enforcers are after him because they think he killed his alpha, but he didn't."

There was a pause before Fyfe had to move the phone away from his ear. Maurice was swearing like a sailor—he'd been one once—and he wasn't quiet about it. "You're friends with James Beltran?"

"I am." Fyfe hadn't known James' surname was Beltran,

but he was pretty sure there weren't two James being accused of killing their alpha at the moment.

"Do you know where he is?"

"No. But he called me, and he told me what was happening. Why haven't the enforcers investigated, Maurice?"

"They have."

Fyfe snorted. "With their feet, maybe. But come on. From what James told me, the entire pack knows the beta killed the alpha, not James. That should be easy enough to prove, shouldn't it? He *is* the one who has the most to gain from of the alpha's death after all. The only thing James got was that he's now on the run, and he's only been a werewolf for a year. You know how dangerous that is. He's not in control."

"That's why you need to get rid of him if he's there, and don't tell me he isn't, Fyfe. I know you."

"Then you know I'm not going to let your guard dogs kill him just because they were told he's a murderer and they don't want to get off their asses long enough to look for the actual killer. And no, he's not here. But like I said, he called me."

"Don't answer his calls anymore. Fyfe, he's going down, whether you like it or not. I don't want you to go down with him. You have to think of yourself and your coven."

Fyfe rubbed his eyes. "I know that. I'm just asking for an investigation. Isn't that the role of the enforcers? They're your armed hand, but they're also supposed to look into this and mete *justice*, not prejudice. I get that some of them are vampires and probably don't care enough about werewolves killing each other, but James is my friend, and he wouldn't hurt a fly."

"I want to ask how you two became friends, but I'm afraid to find out the answer." Maurice sighed. "I'll look into it."

Fyfe straightened. "Thank you."

"Don't thank me yet. I don't know if I can help you, so I'm not promising anything. I'll check in with the leader of the team of enforcers and ask him what's going on, but I doubt I'll get answers you'll like."

"Then assign a new team that's not as biased. Don't you guys have werewolf enforcers?"

"We do. You know that. I'm a vampire, though. The conclave's wolves don't even talk to me. They won't answer to me, either."

"And *that's* one of the major problems the conclave has."

"We've already been through this, and I don't want to hear it again, so cut it, Fyfe. I told you I'll look into it. I don't like the thought of sacrificing an innocent, but I don't know if there's anything I can do to change that."

Maurice was one of the good guys, and Fyfe knew he'd do what he could. He only had limited power, though, just like it should be. The problem was that most of the other conclave members were interested in the job for the power and the money, not because they could help bring justice and making sure innocents didn't pay for things they hadn't done. "But you'll try."

"Of course I will. I hope you know what you're doing, though, Fyfe. Even if James Beltran *is* innocent, he might not be given the benefit of the doubt, and that means that any-one caught helping him will be punished along with him."

"I just gave him an ear and a promise that I'll do what I can to help. That's all."

"We both know you're a terrible liar, even on the phone."

That was probably right, but there was nothing Fyfe could do to change it. "Thank you, Maurice, both for the help and for the incredibly nice compliments."

"Stay out of trouble."

"We both know that's not gonna happen."

"You're going to be the death of me."

"Nah. You've lived through so much. The Pyramids. The dinosaurs. The—" Maurice hung up.

Fyfe snickered. It could have gone better, but it could have gone much worse, too. He couldn't make any promise to James, but he *could* tell him someone was going to help. He wished he could do more, but this was a start—as long as Maurice didn't decide to send a team of enforcers to the coven to grab James.

Fyfe didn't fool himself. Maurice knew exactly where James was, and it was his fault. He really *was* a terrible liar.

He snuck out of the office again and went back to his room. He knew the peace wouldn't last long. He was going to have to deal with the coven members soon, and that meant he had to find a way to explain James' presence. Even if most members wouldn't care about James being a werewolf, they'd still want to know what he was doing with the coven. Fyfe wished he could tell them James wanted to be a coven member, too, and he wanted that to be true, but he knew better. The elders would have his head on a silver platter if he tried that kind of stunt.

He just needed to give himself time, though. He *knew* he could find a way around the elders. There weren't many of them, not who hated him, but of course, those were the ones who would give him trouble.

He had a few days to figure it out, though. James needed rest, so he probably wouldn't be against spending a day or two in bed in Fyfe's room. That was the one room that was off limits for everyone in the coven, so they wouldn't disturb James.

James didn't look like the kind of guy who could stay still for long, and he was going to get angsty and try to leave. He'd already tried that once that Fyfe knew of. He wanted to go because he thought he was putting the coven and Fyfe in danger, and Fyfe liked that about him. He was a victim, yet he was still trying to protect other people.

So Fyfe was going to protect him. He couldn't explain why he wanted to except for the fact that he was drawn to James, that he wanted to get to know him, but then why didn't matter. James was there now, and Fyfe had never stepped back from a difficult situation.

Even when it might mean prison, or worse—death.

CHAPTER THREE

James glared at the wall. There was nothing else he could do. He'd been glaring at the walls for days now.

He rolled onto his stomach and clutched the pillow. It smelled like Fyfe, and surprisingly, it helped settle James. He hated being stuck in Fyfe's bedroom. He wanted to go downstairs, to eat in the kitchen, to cook, to go outside in the garden he could see from the window. He wanted to talk to people who weren't Fyfe. He liked Fyfe, but he missed people. Besides, Fyfe hadn't spent a lot of time with him during the night. He had his job to do, and he needed to be in his office for that, especially when he had coven members coming in and out of the place. They still didn't know James was there.

The door opened. Fyfe had told James that he was the only one allowed in the room, so he wasn't worried. Sure enough, Fyfe's head poked in, and he grinned. "Still in bed?" he asked as he came in. He was wearing a housecoat and a white shirt, and he looked like he belonged in another era, especially with his long dark hair loose over his shoulder.

"What else am I supposed to do?"

Fyfe sighed and closed the door. He leaned against it and looked down at James. "I know this situation isn't ideal—"

"Ideal? It's a mess. I'm a prisoner, as surely as if the conclave had decided to stick me in a cell."

Fyfe's gaze hardened. "But they haven't. No, they've decided to kill you because they can't be bothered to investigate what really happened to your alpha."

James flopped on his back. "I know. I'm sorry. But it's like this . . . this itch under my skin. I need to go out, to run in the forest, or even in your garden."

Fyfe sat on the edge of the mattress and patted James' thigh. It was under a blanket, but Fyfe might as well have been touching James' naked skin. The contact went straight to James' dick, and he rolled to his side to hide the probable erection that was coming.

He should be getting used to the way he reacted to Fyfe's presence, but he wasn't sure he ever would. No one could get under his skin like Fyfe did. Fyfe was funny, smart, and had a huge heart. He was trying to do right by everyone, James included, even though James was nothing to him, especially not next to his coven.

"I know it's not easy," Fyfe said.

James snorted. "It's not."

"But there's nothing else you can do. You're going to have to ignore the wolf for a while longer."

James frowned and sat up, all thoughts of sex and Fyfe naked fleeing from his mind. "What do you mean, ignore the wolf?"

Fyfe gestured toward James. "The wolf. That itch you're feeling. It's the wolf wanting to come out. I guess he likes being locked in just as much as you do."

"It's the wolf?"

"Yes. You didn't know?"

James shook his head. He realized he had a lot to learn about being a werewolf, but he'd thought he'd been making progress, at least until Alpha Torres was killed. It seemed like he hadn't learned much, though. "Can you tell me about this? About werewolves?"

"What do you want to know?"

"Everything."

Fyfe smiled. "If it makes you stay. Okay, like vampires,

werewolves are made. I'm not sure it works like us, but probably not, not entirely. Vampirism is like a disease. You get infected when a vampire secretes the venom and bites you, pushing it into your bloodstream. It takes a bit before you fully turn, an incubation time if you will. As far as I know, werewolves work that way, too. You have a different virus, though, and it can be transmitted to children when they're conceived. That's why your friend Oscar was a born werewolf, as they call it."

"Are born werewolves different?"

"Not that I know of, but werewolves who are born that way are viewed like treasures. There aren't many werewolves around, and they have low natality and high mortality rates. The children who survive to adulthood are even fewer because the wolf takes so much energy to control."

"I know all about that."

Fyfe gently touched James' cheek. "I know you're not in control when the moon is full, or ever, but that's going to change eventually. You'll be able to learn to still be yourself when the moon is full, and even to shift when it isn't. Becoming a werewolf might not have been your choice, but you are one now, and you have to deal with that and learn to like it. There's nothing worse than spending decades or even hundreds of years hating a part of yourself."

He sounded like he spoke from experience. James wanted to ask about it, but if Fyfe wasn't telling him, it meant he didn't want to, that maybe he wasn't ready. They might have spent time talking over the past few days, but it had been about things that didn't really matter, like favorite movies or books, not how Fyfe had become a vampire and why.

"You can teach me?" he asked, hoping the answer would be yes but already knowing it was impossible.

Fyfe pressed his lips together and shook his head. "I can't.

I'm a vampire. I don't feel the same pull from the moon, the same need to give in to another part of myself. I'm just me all of the time, even though I'm not human anymore."

"I need to learn control." Because if James somehow managed to stay hidden until the next full moon, he was going to have to find a safe place in the coven's home to shift, and he knew there wasn't one. The coven didn't need that kind of place, and that was one thing James wasn't going to compromise on. He wasn't going to hurt anyone. He'd never forgive himself if he did.

"You will."

James pushed Fyfe's hand away. "How? You can't teach me, and I can't leave this place. Where am I going to find a werewolf ready to help me?" He already knew the answer to that question—he wasn't going to.

The only person who'd agreed to do that was dead. No one else in the pack had wanted to bother. Maybe it was because they'd known all along that he was going to be a scapegoat, or maybe it was because they didn't like him, or they didn't care. Whatever the reason, James hadn't been able to learn control, and he knew he wasn't going to until he found someone who could help.

That wasn't going to happen if he stayed with the coven.

Even if his name was cleared, even if the coven accepted him instead of rejecting him, all of them were vampires. They couldn't teach him this.

He needed to leave, and the sooner he did, the better it would be for the coven. "I'll go."

Fyfe cocked his head. "What?"

"Tomorrow, while you're sleeping. I'll leave. I know you want to help, but like you said, you can't, not with this, and I'm not about to wait to see if I hurt someone."

"You're not going to."

"You can't know that. I can't control my shift of the wolf

inside me. That's dangerous."

Fyfe rubbed his face. "Okay. I get what you're saying, and you're not wrong. You can't leave, though. The conclave might find you."

"I managed to stay away from them for a while. I can continue doing it."

"They'll eventually get to you. We both know that. Please, James. Let me call Maurice back and see if he found anything. At least let me try. If he can't help, you and I can talk and find another way out. I'm not going to throw you to the wolves, though. The pack might have done that, but I'm not like them."

"Fyfe . . ."

"And you're comfortable enough here, right? I understand you want to go outside, but you have food and warm water to shower, and clean clothes. Surely all those things will be enough for another few days. I promise that if I don't find anything useful, I'll let you leave then."

James wanted to say yes, but it would be foolish. He needed to leave, and he needed to do it as soon as Fyfe left. He'd be busy with his work and wouldn't notice James was missing for at least a few hours.

James nodded and forced himself to smile. He was going to miss Fyfe, but this was the best thing he could do, for everyone.

Fyfe couldn't focus, but then, he hadn't been able to focus since James had barged into his life in all his furry, naked glory. Fyfe doubted that would change anytime soon, too. He'd panicked when James had told him he wanted to leave.

He knew it would be the best for everyone, except maybe for James, but maybe even for him. The coven would be safe from the conclave, and James wouldn't get caught and might be able to find another werewolf who could teach him control. Fyfe had been calling all the friendly wolves he could think of, but the one he really wanted to help James wasn't in town right now, and he didn't trust any of the others enough to tell them about James.

He also still hadn't heard from Maurice, and he dreaded it. He was going to have to call since he'd promised James he would, but he already knew what Maurice's silence meant. He might still be digging and questioning people, but it wasn't going well.

"Stop him!"

The sound of a scuffle made Fyfe jerk. He looked at the door and frowned, hoping it wasn't Andrew and Falkner again. He'd already separated them once this week, and if they were still fighting, he'd put them in time out this time. He had enough on his plate not to want to police two grown men who behaved like children.

"Filthy—"

Fyfe frowned. That didn't sound like Andrew or Falkner. Even if they were fighting, they wouldn't insult each other. No one in the coven would say that kind of thing to another coven member.

But they would to James.

Fyfe's stomach turned to lead, and he tripped on the leg of his desk in his hurry to get to the door. Goddammit. Had James really been so stupid to try to sneak out during the night, when everyone in the house was awake? Fyfe could see it happening. James had a noble soul, and the fact that he was putting Fyfe and everyone else in the coven in danger just by sticking around had weighed on him since day one.

So Fyfe wasn't surprised when he got to the entrance and saw two of the guards dragging James back, away from the door. James' backpack had been thrown in the corner, and James looked like he might be shifting any second. He wouldn't be in control if he did, though, and he might hurt someone. Then he'd hate himself for it because he was that kind of guy.

"What's happening here?" Fyfe asked, his voice booming in the space around him. He was terrified, but he'd long learned not to expose that kind of feeling on his face. The coven would never know that he was afraid for James, not unless he wanted them to.

Aubrey, one of the guards, pushed James toward the stairs. Fyfe wanted to rush down, and he realized he was moving faster than he normally would. He needed to get to James, though. He needed to make sure James was okay.

"We caught this one sneaking in."

"I wasn't sneaking in!" James protested. He was on his knees at the foot of the stairs with one arm folded behind his back. Aubrey held it, and Fyfe knew he wouldn't let go until he was ordered to.

Fyfe glared at James. No, he wasn't sneaking in. He was sneaking out, and Fyfe wanted to beat his ass for it. Hadn't they talked about this half an hour ago? "Silence," he growled.

He didn't miss the triumphant scowl the guard sent James' way. He didn't care.

"Shall I take him to the cell?" Aubrey asked.

"No. Get up, James. Aubrey, let him go."

Aubrey blinked, but he obeyed. He stepped back, and Fyfe finished walking down the stairs. He held his hand out, his heart beating faster when James took it and allowed him to pull him up. There were gasps and swearing around them—part of the coven had heard the scuffle and was now gathered in the entrance—but no one said anything.

Yet.

It wasn't going to last, of course, but it gave Fyfe a moment to make sure James was okay. "Are you hurt?"

James shook his head. "Just my pride. I thought I could leave without anyone noticing me."

"Just because I managed to sneak you *in* doesn't mean you could sneak out. I know where the guards are. I'm the one who makes that kind of decision. You're not."

Fyfe *knew* everyone was gaping. He didn't care. He made sure James was steady on his feet and gave him a quick look over to check whether he was okay. He couldn't see any open wounds, but if he knew his people—and he did—they'd probably been rough. They'd seen him as an intruder, and it was something they took seriously.

"Fyfe?" Aubrey asked, his voice strangled.

Fyfe sighed. He'd wanted to plan this moment. He should have known better, though. When did anything go the way he wanted it to?

He stood straighter and looked around, almost groaning when he noticed Alfred, one of the elders of the coven, in a corner. He was scowling, which was a normal Alfred expression. Fyfe wasn't going to let anyone intimidate him, though. "James will be staying with us for a while."

There were gasps and whispers—everyone could tell James was a werewolf from his scent, and they'd never had to share the house with anyone who wasn't a vampire. "He's a werewolf," Falkner said. He was hovering close to Andrew, and Fyfe was happy to see they weren't fighting this time. One crisis at a time was more than enough for him.

"I know. And we're vampires. All of us have heard about the wars vampires and werewolves used to get into, and we've been taught to hate them. But James has never done anything to hurt any of you. I won't tolerate intolerance or hate, not in this coven. Most of us were outcasts at one point. You know what that feels like. I expect you to be accepting of James. Even if you don't want to be his friend or to talk to him, none of you will be cruel to him."

"Is that an order, leader?" Alfred said.

He was still scowling.

Fyfe knew he had to tread carefully here. He was the leader, so his words were law, but this was Alfred. He was one of the few who'd never fully accepted Fyfe's leadership, even though he always made a show of being respectful while at the same time adding scorn to his voice. He and the few others on his side didn't have a lot of power, but they could still complicate things, especially if Fyfe let them win. "It is. I'm the one who makes the decisions of who stays with the coven."

"He's a werewolf. You're too young to remember, but—"

"But nothing, Alfred. Yes, I *am* young compared to you. That doesn't mean I'm an idiot. I wouldn't have offered James a place to stay if I wasn't sure he was a good man. A *safe* man." Fyfe looked around again. "I've never put restrictions on who you can be friends with, or even on who you bring into the coven to visit. I won't allow anyone trying to do it to me."

Alfred tsked. "The way you talk makes it sound like he's more than a friend to you."

Fyfe hadn't meant to be so transparent, especially when James had no idea how he felt about him. Hell, *Fyfe* wasn't sure what he felt about James. He just knew he believed him and wanted to keep him safe. He hadn't allowed himself to examine the reasons behind that yet, though.

But it was a good explanation. Someone might come up with a good reason for James to leave if he was only a friend, but if James was Fyfe's lover? His boyfriend? Well, that reason wouldn't work because of course Fyfe would want his lover with him. And since he'd never forbidden anyone from having a lover over, even when they'd been humans or from another species, no one would be able to do it to him. "That's because he is," Fyfe declared.

He rolled his eyes at the renewed gasps. He'd thought his coven knew him better than this. How was it surprising?

Fyfe straightened. "James is my lover, and you will treat him as such. He deserves respect, even if you don't agree with his presence here."

James blinked. He hadn't heard that right, had he? Because there was no way Fyfe had just told what had to be at least half the coven that he and James were an item.

The old man, who didn't look that old, made a face, as if he'd just stepped into dog shit. "Are you serious, Leader? You debased yourself with that dog?"

James wasn't going to punch the asshole, and he wasn't going to let his werewolf out to take a bite out of him, either.

He was going to do his best anyway. He couldn't be sure a hundred percent that he'd be able to control his wolf, though, not when his human side wanted his own pound of old flesh.

Fyfe snarled. "I will *not* tolerate this kind of talk from *anyone* in the coven, Alfred, and that includes you. I don't care that you're an elder. As one, you should show leadership, not be an asshole."

Alfred's cheeks flushed, and he gritted his teeth so hard James thought he heard the bones crack, even from where he was.

Good. Let Alfred break a tooth or two.

"Leader, I—"

"I don't want to hear it. You made what you think clear. I don't have to answer to you, not when it comes to my personal life, and you should remember that."

"Your personal life has to come after the coven, especially when it could endanger us."

"It won't."

"He's a werewolf."

"And like I said, you're an asshole. There hasn't been a war between the wolves and the vampires in hundreds of years. You need to get over your hatred, and if you don't, you at least need to keep quiet about it. And that *is* an order."

Alfred huffed and turned around, stomping away.

James wasn't sure what to do or say. He'd thought he was going to make it out the door before anyone noticed he was there, but he'd been caught, and now there he was, Fyfe's fake lover.

Shit. What if the conclave found out about this? What if they heard about Fyfe having a werewolf lover and came to investigate? They normally wouldn't—what people did in their bedrooms wasn't their business unless it wasn't consensual—but they were hunting a werewolf right now.

They were hunting *him.*

Fyfe waved. "Go on, everyone. Get back to what you were doing. I'll be in my office later if you have questions or need something, but it better not have anything to do with my love life. Like I told Alfred, it's my business, and only mine. I can understand some of you are wary about James' presence here, but I can assure you that I wouldn't have brought him in if I hadn't trusted him. He's a good man, and you'll realize that if you give him a chance." Fyfe stared at the crowd that had formed until it started to disband.

James knew that wasn't the end of it. Some of the people were gathering in small groups, looking at him and Fyfe and muttering under their breaths. James couldn't tell if they were taking this well, and he told himself not to panic. Even if they hated him on principle for what he was, they wouldn't think to go to the conclave. *Right?*

Fyfe pinched the bridge of his nose. "That could have gone better."

James climbed the step that still separated them and leaned closer. "Why did you do that?"

Fyfe shook his head. "Not here." He grabbed James' hand and pulled him upstairs. "Come on."

"My backpack."

"It'll still be here when we're done talking. Don't worry. No one is going to touch it, except maybe to take it to my bedroom."

James *was* worried. That bag held everything he owned, and he didn't want to lose it. He realized Fyfe was probably right, though. Even if someone noticed it, they'd be able to smell James on it, and if they didn't want repercussions, they'd make sure James got it back.

Or he hoped so anyway. He could say goodbye to it if Alfred was the one who noticed it.

"Wait!" someone said behind James as he and Fyfe climbed the stairs.

A man rushed up the stairs, James' bag in his hand. He looked down when he handed it to James. "Here, I thought you'd like to have this."

James looked at Fyfe, unsure of what to say. Was being the leader's fake lover a special position? Did it give him power over the coven? God, he hoped not. He didn't even have enough control to keep his wolf in check, let alone an entire coven.

Fyfe smiled. "Thank you, Archie."

Archie smiled. "I just wanted to say that I don't care. I know that when we talked in the laundry room, I wasn't exactly nice about, well, werewolves, but you're right. James didn't do anything to me, and I shouldn't judge him for what others did to me."

"Thanks, Archie. I'm glad to hear that." Fyfe pointedly looked at James and cleared his throat.

James wasn't sure what to say, so he settled on *thank you*

and scampered behind Fyfe back to his room. He supposed having at least one ally was a good thing, but he couldn't help but wonder what Archie would say if he knew what was really happening. Would he believe the conclave and think James was a ruthless killer? Or would he give him the benefit of the doubt like Fyfe had?

Fyfe locked his bedroom door when they got there and leaned against it. "Okay, I should probably have thought this through better, and I definitely should have talked to you about it before telling everyone you were my lover."

James snorted and dumped his bag on the bed. "Yeah, you should have."

"But on the other hand, you promised you wouldn't leave until I'd had the chance to call Maurice, yet you were caught sneaking out."

James shrugged. "I thought I was doing the right thing. I still do. I don't think me staying here is a good idea. We both know the conclave is going to find me sooner or later, and then the coven will be in trouble. And with the fact that you told everyone we're together, *you* will take most of the hit if something happens."

Fyfe pursed his lips. "You're not wrong. I've been dealing with the conclave for a while, though, so don't worry too much about me. I don't regret what I said."

"You will." Eventually. Everyone regretted being in contact with James. Well, except the people who died, like Alpha Torres.

Fyfe crossed his arms over his chest. "Nope. And this way, you can't sneak out again."

"I can't?"

"You're my boyfriend now. That means we stick together."

"It's not real, though."

Fyfe licked his lips, and James' gaze went to them without

his consent. He couldn't say he hadn't thought about kissing Fyfe and what it would be like about a hundred times since Fyfe had taken him in, but this was different.

"It could be," Fyfe said.

There were a lot of promises in his voice, and James wanted to hold him to all of them.

He couldn't. "I could hurt someone. I can't stay here."

Fyfe huffed. "Of course you can. And you haven't hurt anyone since you got here."

"That's because the full moon is over. But if I'm not chained to a wall in a deserted place next month, I could."

"You can't believe that chaining yourself is the best way to deal with this."

"I know it's not, but I don't exactly have an alternative. I don't know anyone who could teach me control. The pack didn't, and they should have. Why should anyone else? I'm not their responsibility, and if the conclave finds me . . ."

"Can you just stop thinking about the conclave for a moment?"

"Oh, sorry if me being worried about making it out of this alive is annoying you," James snapped.

Fyfe jerked back, and James regretted it, but he didn't apologize. He needed Fyfe to understand, and he wasn't sure how to make that happen.

"I'm sorry," Fyfe said. "I know this is hard for you. I've never been through anything like this, but like I said, I've dealt with the conclave often enough to know them and the way they behave. I want to compromise, okay? You'll stay here until the full moon, and I'll try to sort things out. If I haven't made any progress by then, you'll leave and go chain yourself somewhere, and I won't try to stop you."

"You promise?"

"I promise."

And for some reason, James believed him.

Fyfe needed to do something. He had to get James out of trouble, find him someone who could teach him control, and make sure he was happy with the coven. That was the only way he'd get James to stay.

So he called Maurice. One day, the man was going to stop answering his phone when he saw it was Fyfe, but thankfully, today was not that day.

"What do you want?" Maurice asked gruffly.

"To find out if you had news."

Maurice sighed. Fyfe could almost see him in his office, leaning back in his chair and rubbing his eyes like he always did when he was tired—which was most of the time. They didn't see each other often, but they *knew* each other. "Yes and no."

"That doesn't sound good." And Fyfe was glad he'd left James in the bedroom when he'd decided to call from his office.

"Well, the wolves on the conclave are pushing for this to be resolved. One of them was Alpha Torres' wife's cousin or whatever, but he thinks it makes them family and that he'll look weak if he doesn't make sure James pays."

"Even if he didn't do anything?"

"He just wants this out of the way. He's not particular about who pays, as long as someone does and he can boast about it."

That wasn't what Fyfe had wanted to hear. "What can I do? The coven found out about James."

"The coven? I thought he wasn't with you?"

Damn it. "He's not. But they noticed I was behaving weirdly, and I told them I was dating a werewolf."

"*What?*"

Fyfe shrugged even though Maurice couldn't see him.

"Why not? They're used to me being weird."

"Weird, yes, but not a reckless fool. Do you know what will happen to you if the rest of the conclave finds out you're dating a werewolf convicted of murder?"

"*Was* he convicted? Because from what he told me, the pack decided he was guilty and handed him off to the enforcers, who then decided to cut his head off. That doesn't sound like a conviction to me."

"You know what I mean. What the conclave says, goes, unless you have solid proof otherwise."

Fyfe sighed. He wanted to kick something until the frustration disappeared, but he knew better than to ruin perfectly good furniture. "I don't."

"Which is where I come in. I haven't been able to do much, but I know what team is hunting your man, and I know that one of the members will do what he can to make sure James doesn't pay if he's not guilty. It's not a promise that everything is going to be okay, but it's something."

Fyfe wished Maurice could work miracles, but this was better than nothing. "Who's this guy?"

"Ignatius."

"Ah." Fyfe remembered Ignatius. They'd had a fling a few hundred years ago. It had ended amicably, but they hadn't talked much since then, and Fyfe wasn't sure how he'd take a help request from him.

"That's all you have to say? *Ah?*"

"I know him."

"I'm aware of that."

"What did he say?" Fyfe wasn't sure what to expect considering his now non-existent relationship with Ignatius.

"That he'd look into it."

"I see." Fyfe supposed it was better than nothing.

"Oh, don't thank me too much, Fyfe. I only did what I thought was right."

Fyfe laughed. "I'm sorry, Maurice. Thank you very much for this. I know you didn't have to and that it would have been easier for you to look the other way."

Maurice sighed. "But it wouldn't have been right. Do you have Ignatius' number?"

"No."

"I'll text it to you. I don't think I can do anything else, Fyfe, not right now. Unless Ignatius finds proof that James is being framed, it's out of my hands. If he does, though, he'll contact me, and I'll revoke the order to capture James."

"Thank you." It was more than Fyfe had let himself hope.

He called Ignatius as soon as he and Maurice hung up and Maurice texted him. He was a bit nervous—he'd never had to ask this big a favor from one of his exes, and he had quite a few of them, considering how old he was. He supposed he was lucky the relationship with Ignatius had ended relatively well. He'd be in trouble if he had to ask favors from some of his other exes. He'd tried to kill a few of them.

"Who is this?" Ignatius snapped when he answered.

Fyfe leaned back in his chair and tried to relax. "That's not the best way to greet an old lover, Igni." As far as Fyfe knew, he was the only one to call Ignatius that, so he hoped his ex would recognize him.

"I already told you not to call me that. I have a name."

Fyfe grinned. "And it's complicated."

"It really isn't. what do you want, Fyfe?"

"I might just want to talk."

"We both know that's a lie. I can hang up if you don't want to tell me."

"No, please." Fyfe licked his lips. This was it. If Ignatius told him to fuck off, he'd have to find another way to help James, and he wasn't sure one existed at this point. "I need a favor."

"I suspected that was the case."

"I know you're working right now. You're trying to find and capture a werewolf."

"It's not a secret." Ignatius' voice was slightly wary now. They hadn't been together long, but they'd been friends before becoming lovers, and they knew each other. Even the decades hadn't changed Fyfe so much Ignatius wouldn't recognize him.

"I need you to *actually* investigate the death of Alpha Torres."

"Are you telling me how to do my job?" Ignatius asked. His voice was tinged with anger, and that was the last thing Fyfe wanted.

"Of course not. I'm sure you're great at what you do. But I know the conclave, and I know you probably can't always do things the way you want to do them. Most of the members are more worried about what they get out of any given situation than what's right."

There was a pause, and Fyfe prayed Ignatius would at least listen to him. He didn't believe in God anymore, hadn't for a long time, but sometimes, he fell back into old patterns. The fact that James was the reason for it was a big clue as to what Fyfe felt for him.

"I'm listening," Ignatius said.

"I . . . might have talked with James recently."

"What the fuck, Fyfe? Do you know where he is?"

"No."

"I don't believe you."

"You're going to have to do with that answer, though, because it's the only one you'll get."

Ignatius huffed. "Fine."

"Like I said, I talked to him, and his version is pretty different from what the enforcers were told."

"Of course it is."

"Listen to me, please. He says he was used as a scapegoat.

The beta and other people weren't happy that Alpha Torres had taken him in. When they decided to kill the alpha, they used James. He didn't do anything."

"How can you be sure? Are you friends with James?"

"No. We met recently. But I trust my guts when it comes to people, and you know I'm usually right. I was about you."

"What do you want me to do? I can't promise you I'll be able to prove he's innocent."

"No, but you can investigate and find what actually happened. The beta killed the alpha to take his place, and he can't have been the only one in on it."

"And if more than one person knew about it, there has to be a weak link."

"Exactly. I don't expect you to believe what James has to say, but I know you. You want to do what's right. That's why you work for the conclave, isn't it?"

Ignatius sighed. "It's not what I expected, not anymore."

"But you can change that. Helping James might not make a big difference, but it would be one more innocent man still alive because you did what you thought was right. Please. If you don't want to do it because of that, do it for me. I know we're not really friends anymore, but—"

"I'll do it, Fyfe. And we *are* friends. I'll come by the next time I'm in town. I just hope for your sake it won't be for a while, and I'm going to ignore the feeling I have that James is holed up with you. I won't steer the rest of the team away, though. If they decide to come your way, I'll let them. But I'll go back to the pack and see what I can find out."

"Talk to a man named Oscar. He and James were friends. He might know something." Fyfe didn't want to give Oscar away as the person who'd let James go, but he hoped Oscar *did* know something, especially with the beta being his father.

"I will. Don't hold your breath, though. It's not looking good for James Beltran."

Chapter Four

Everyone was watching him.

James knew it sounded paranoid, but it was true. Everyone in the house stared and watched every time he left Fyfe's bedroom, and he wasn't sure why. Was it because he was a werewolf, or because he was Fyfe's lover? The reason didn't really matter, he supposed. Whatever it was, it didn't change the fact that they hated him.

James licked his lips. He was hungry, and Fyfe had told him he'd bought some food and had left it for him in the kitchen. Fyfe had brought it to him until now, and he hadn't protested about it, but James knew he couldn't keep on relying on him. The man was busy with his job and trying to find a way for James to be declared innocent and freed, so the less James bothered him, the better it was.

That meant he was going to have to face the coven, or at the very least, the members who would be in the kitchen when he got there.

He'd purposefully waited until dawn to go downstairs. The coven was more active during the night, and he'd started following their timetable. It was going to suck once he had to leave and get back to a normal schedule, but in the meantime, it was better this way. He'd never get to see and talk to Fyfe otherwise. It would probably be easier for him to sleep during the night so he'd have the entire house to himself during the day, but he couldn't bring himself to do that.

He liked Fyfe. He'd stopped trying to convince himself otherwise several days ago. How could he not feel anything for the one man who was trying to help him? The one man who believed he wasn't a monster, no matter what he was? And it wasn't only that. Fyfe was helping him, but he was also a man James could easily fall in love with.

It was obvious he didn't want to be the coven leader, yet he'd never spoken of stepping down. He knew he was the coven's best bet to survive and thrive, and he made sure the members were safe and could do what they wanted with their lives. He cared for them, even when they were disrespectful like Alfred had been when James had been discovered. He dedicated most of his time to the coven, and he was always available for whoever needed to talk. He was considerate, calm, and he thought about everything before making decisions.

The fact that he was hot as fuck didn't make things easier on James, either. James wanted to run his hands through Fyfe's long, dark hair. He wanted to see how it would feel on his skin. He wanted to trace the tattoos he got peeks of when Fyfe came to bed, before they turned off the light and settled down for the day. He wanted to know what having Fyfe on top of him felt like, maybe even *inside* him. He hadn't let himself fall for anyone or have sex with anyone when he'd been with the pack because it had been obvious to him that they weren't exactly tolerant, and it was starting to weigh on him with Fyfe so close.

James suspected Fyfe would be enthusiastic at the thought of having sex. He wasn't discreet about the fact that he liked James, even though he'd never pushed him into anything. No, he was letting James guide the show, and he was going to continue that way, so it was James' decision, really. James wasn't sure he could take it, though. It would be easy to try to forget what was happening to him in Fyfe's arms, to drown his worries in Fyfe's body, but all his problems would still be there when the moon became full again.

He didn't have much time left with the coven, and he wasn't sure how he felt about that.

He snuck out of the bedroom and made his way downstairs. Considering how everyone behaved with him, he wouldn't mind having another place to stay. It would make things easier for everyone. He'd be away from Fyfe, though, and since that thought was painful on its own, it meant Fyfe already meant much more to James than James had wanted him to. He was going to have to do something about it once he went, but he had so little time left. Surely, he could let himself enjoy Fyfe's company for a few more days?

The house wasn't dark yet. James could hear voices down in the wing where the bedrooms were, and since he was going the other way, it was perfect. He was silent as he climbed down the stairs, not turning on lights. He didn't need them to see, and he didn't want anyone to notice him.

The lack of light was one of the reasons he didn't notice the two men in the kitchen when he stepped in.

They were tucked in the breakfast nook with their heads close together as they kissed. James looked away, but it was too late. The one facing him had already noticed him, and he moved away from the other, looking like he wasn't quite sure what to do.

James cleared his throat. "Sorry for interrupting. I just wanted something to eat."

"Uh, sure. Fyfe said he'd bought you stuff, I think."

"He did. I'm just gonna . . ." James waved toward the fridge. He still wasn't sure why the coven owned one, or a kitchen that would have looked at home in one of those magazines for furniture stores.

"Yeah, of course."

This was awkward. James knew who the guys were—he'd noticed them that day in the entrance, and they always seemed to be hanging around, always together. That made sense now that he'd caught them kissing, but he wasn't friends with them, so he wasn't going to say anything about that.

He quickly put together a sandwich, put everything back in the fridge, and made for the door, but before he could leave, Andrew cleared his throat, so he paused.

"Could you not tell anyone about this?" he asked.

James frowned. "About what?"

"That you saw us kissing."

James wasn't sure why it should be a problem or why he should talk about it to anyone, but it wasn't his business. "Of course." He was curious, though. "You know Fyfe wouldn't care, right?"

Andrew and Falkner looked at each other. They did that silent communication thing James had seen so many times between couples and longed to have. He sighed. It would be better for him to stop thinking about that kind of thing, especially when he wanted it with Fyfe.

"We know," Andrew confirmed. "But Fyfe isn't the only one we have to deal with."

"Ah. Others would have a problem with the two of you?" James wasn't surprised, considering some of the reactions he'd gotten.

"Yeah, and we don't want Fyfe to be in trouble because he's progressive. He already has enough problems with you being here." He winced. "Sorry. I didn't mean that."

James shrugged. "Yeah, you did, and you're right. I told Fyfe I wanted to leave because it would make things easier for everyone, but he's stubborn."

Falkner chuckled. "That's right. And, well, sorry for not being friendly. I mean, you're Fyfe's boyfriend, so we should have welcomed you, but, well . . ."

"But I'm a werewolf, and you don't know me. I get it. And no worries. I haven't been the friendliest person either."

He wished he had, but he knew it was better this way. He was going to leave soon, and he probably wouldn't come back. Making friends just to leave them wasn't a good plan.

The thought of going back to Fyfe's bedroom was stifling. James peeked outside, smiling when he saw that dawn was just barely visible at the horizon. He'd be left alone if he went outside. The house Fyfe and the coven lived in was gorgeous, and so was the garden around it. It wouldn't be a hardship to spend some time outside, even though the air was nippy.

James took his sandwich outside after bundling himself into a blanket he'd found in the living room. He hoped its owner wouldn't mind. It would probably smell of werewolf once he was done with it.

There was a bench on the side of the house. James would be left alone there, so he sat, cross-legged, and ate his sandwich while thinking that this was probably the last quiet and comfortable moment he'd have for a while—or ever. He didn't know what was going to happen when the conclave caught up with him, but he knew they would, and that it wasn't going to be pretty.

Fyfe glared at the wall. "I understand we're not friends, but—"

"But nothing. You're a bloodsucker. I'm not going to help you," the man growled on the other side of the phone.

"It's not me you need to help. James is a werewolf, like you. He needs to learn control. You know that."

"I also know he lives with you, so my answer is still no. I don't want anything to do with bloodsuckers or anyone who associates with your creepy asses."

He hung up. Fyfe had to resist the urge to throw his phone at the wall. He needed it, so he couldn't afford to be without it the time it took to buy a new one.

He'd promised James he would help him, and so far, he hadn't managed to do anything for him. He hadn't found anyone to help him learn control, which meant he was going to leave soon. He hadn't heard back from Ignatius, so as far as the conclave was aware, James was still guilty, and they were still hunting him. The only thing Fyfe had done was to delay the inevitable.

He slammed his phone down on his desk and rubbed his face. He needed to go to bed. It was nearly dawn, and he'd worked too late. James was going to wonder where he was, and Fyfe wanted to spend the few days they still had together with him.

The house was mostly silent by now, but Fyfe heard giggles coming up the stairs. He paused and waited to see who it was, grinning when Falkner and Andrew stumbled onto the landing, their hands linked together. Andrew turned and pressed against Falkner, kissing him, and while Fyfe didn't usually mind watching people having sex, this was different. Those two were his charges, and he cared for them too much.

He cleared his throat. Andrew and Falkner both jumped, and when they saw Fyfe, the sprung apart. Andrew rubbed his hands on his thighs, his eyes wide. "Fyfe? It's not what you think."

Fyfe rolled his eyes. "Really? Because to me, it seemed like the two of you were making out. I probably interrupted something, but if you want to continue and go to your room for the night, feel free."

They looked at each other. "We don't . . . ."

Fyfe didn't need this. God, was he such a bad leader that Andrew and Falkner were afraid of telling him they were together? Why, for fuck's sake? He'd told them and everyone else in the coven that he and James were together. Why did they think he'd have a problem with them? "You know I don't care, right?" he asked.

Falkner licked his lips. "We didn't know."

"James and I are together."

"Yeah, but it's not the same thing. You're the leader."

There was more to this, Fyfe could tell. He didn't think Andrew and Falkner were going to tell him right now, though. "It *is* the same thing, so don't bother hiding it from me. I want to see the two of you tomorrow, in my office. Come whenever you want. We'll talk about this."

Falkner paled. "Fyfe—"

"Not in a bad way, Falkner. Relax. I don't care that the two of you are in love, or fucking, or whatever you're doing."

"Oh. All right. We'll see you tomorrow?"

"Yes."

"He's in the garden, by the way."

Fyfe frowned. "Who?"

"James. He came down to the kitchen earlier and made himself a sandwich. We're sorry we haven't been more accepting of him, Fyfe. If he's the guy you love, we don't care that he's a werewolf. You deserve to be happy and with who you want."

Fyfe's chest tightened. Sometimes he hated being the coven leader, but at times like these, when he realized he wasn't only the leader but also part of a family, he was glad he'd accepted the job. "Thank you. I'll go find him. See you tomorrow, and sleep well." Fyfe winked. "If you sleep at all, of course."

Falkner's cheeks flushed, and Andrew laughed. Fyfe hadn't achieved much today, but seeing those two feeling better and more secure was all he needed.

He went downstairs and crossed the living room to go outside, but he was once again stopped before he could.

"Leader?"

Fyfe almost groaned. He *did* groan, although he kept the sound inside, and turned toward Alfred. "What can I do for you, Alfred?"

No one knew how old Alfred was. Fyfe had never asked, and he didn't want to know. He looked old, though. He'd been bitten when he was in his late fifties, and that was how he'd look forever. The fact that he never smiled and didn't apparently care for grooming and self-care didn't help, either.

"You need to make him leave."

Fyfe blinked. "I'm sorry?"

"The dog. He needs to leave. This isn't a place for him. We're a coven of vampires. We have to follow certain rules and traditions, and—"

"Rules?"

Alfred nodded. "And traditions, yes. I realize you're young, but this is how we've always done things here."

Fyfe crossed his arms over his chest. "You mean before me. That's how you've always done things here before I came along and killed your leader."

Alfred's back went ramrod straight. "I know he wasn't the best person, but—"

"I had to pry him off the body of one of the coven members, Alfred. He killed her because she didn't want to have sex with him."

"He was our leader. She should have obeyed his orders."

Fyfe really wanted to punch something right now. "You mean the way *you* are obeying me right now?"

Alfred's cheeks flushed. "I'm just trying to make sure the coven stays the way it's always been."

"Why should it? The fact that we're not aging doesn't mean we should stay the same way we were when we were turned, Alfred. The world outside this house is changing, and we need to change with it if we don't want to be left be-hind. I understand I'm not going to change your mind, but you have a choice. You can stay here and listen to me, obey my orders, and let me lead the coven the way I see fit, or you can leave and find a coven that fits you better. Or of course, you can challenge me for the leadership." But they both knew Alfred wouldn't win, not in a fair fight.

It didn't have to be fair, though. Alfred clearly wanted James out, and Fyfe wouldn't put it past him to contact the conclave. He could tell them Fyfe was letting James lead the coven, or that Fyfe was making decisions he shouldn't be making, and the conclave would investigate. There were both vampire and werewolf members on the conclave, but that didn't mean they didn't agree with Alfred or that they accepted mixed couples and covens or packs.

No matter what Fyfe was saying, he and Alfred both knew Alfred could create a lot of problems and possibly have Fyfe removed as the leader. What would happen then? Fyfe knew what kind of man Alfred was. He'd lived with him long enough and had listened to him when he ranted about traditions not being respected. If he were ever in charge, he'd take the coven back hundreds of years. He'd want the women to be submissive. He'd want to be the one to decided who married whom. He'd ruin the coven Fyfe had worked so hard for.

And worse, he'd hand James over to the conclave, and that wasn't something Fyfe was ready to think about.

Fyfe rubbed his face. He was letting emotions cloud his judgment, and he shouldn't. James had become important to him, though, and he doubted he could get over that. He needed to keep both the coven safe—and possibly get rid of Alfred—and to make sure James made it out of this shitty situation alive, in one piece, and in control.

Where the fuck was he supposed to start?

Removing James from the coven was probably the best first step to take. Fyfe hated even thinking about it, but if Alfred called the conclave, they'd come, and no one would be able to stop them. So Fyfe needed to get James to a safe place. That way Alfred wouldn't have a reason to call the conclave, or at least Fyfe hoped so. It would also help keep James hidden. He'd been with the coven for a while now, and the word was bound to get out soon.

He didn't want James to leave, but he was going to have to, and Fyfe needed to find him another safe place to stay.

James sighed when he heard the door open. He wasn't sure how long he'd been in the garden, but it felt good, and his wolf was calmer now that he'd left the house for a bit.

"Are you trying to hide?" Fyfe asked.

"Nah. I know you can find me easily. The house is big, but it's not that big, especially with all the rooms that are off limits."

"Only the private bedrooms."

"I know."

Fyfe flopped down on the bench next to James. He was always so graceful when he moved, and James wondered if it was him or if the vampirism had transformed him. He hadn't noticed many changes in his human self since he'd been bitten and had become a werewolf, but it had only been a year. Would he still be this way in fifty or sixty years? Or would he become more like the wolf?

"You need to leave, James."

James' heart felt like it tripped. He knew he had to leave. He'd been planning to leave. But hearing it from Fyfe hurt, much more than it should have. They were friends, but that was it. Right? "I know."

"I've already found another safe place. I wish I could keep

you here and I want you to come back as soon as this mess is solved, but right now, you'll be safer away from the coven. Alfred is getting antsy, and I expect him to start something. I'm not sure what yet, but I'd feel better if you weren't here when it happens, just in case it involves the conclave or trying to take the leadership from me."

James twisted on the bench so he could see Fyfe. "Is that a possibility? Is he going to try for the leadership?"

"Well, we both know I'd win in a fair fight. But Alfred is one of the old guard, and by that, I mean that he was a strong supporter of the old leader. He's crafty and won't stop for anything to get what he wants. I'm still not sure why he stayed instead of leaving when I became the leader, and honestly, I don't care. I'm going to kick his ass if he tries anything, but I can't risk you."

Fyfe cared. That much was obvious, even to James. He wouldn't have risked himself and his coven if he didn't care about James and what happened to him.

And James didn't want to go. "I can find a safe place, don't worry."

Fyfe frowned. "I already did. We have to leave before dawn, though."

"You've already done so much for me, Fyfe. I don't want you to get into more trouble."

Fyfe waved. "I'll be the judge of what's trouble, okay? I want to do this, and I will. I have a safe place, and I'm still trying to find a wolf who will teach you control."

"I don't know what to say." James swallowed. He didn't want to ask this, but it might be the last time he was alone with Fyfe. Hell, it might be the last time he saw Fyfe, period. No one could know how things would go, and he didn't want to die regretting too much.

Fyfe patted James' thigh. "Don't say anything. I told you I'd protect you, and I will. I keep my promises."

"Why?"

Fyfe cocked his head. "Why do I keep my promises?"

"No. Why are you doing all this for me?"

"Because you're my friend."

"And you'd do this for all your friends?"

"Well, yes. Although I have to admit you're kind of special."

"Am I?"

"Yes."

"Why?"

"I don't know. You're young, but I've lived a long time. I've learned that when people are special, when they catch my attention, I need to follow that. I don't want to have regrets."

That was so close to what James had been thinking. He leaned closer to Fyfe, not sure what he was doing. He needed to do *something*, though. He needed to show Fyfe that he was as special to James as James was to him. He wasn't sure how, but he'd find a way. He always did.

Fyfe's lips stretched into a broad smile when he noticed James moving. He pressed closer, until their upper chests brushed against each other and James could feel Fyfe's breath on his skin. "What are you doing, pup?" Fyfe asked, his voice curling around James and making him *want*.

"I'm not sure."

"Mmm. I see. We'll have to make sure you know, then." He stroked a hand up James' arm and hooked it behind James' neck. He gently pulled.

James went. He'd been waiting—*hoping*—for this to happen since almost the first time he'd seen Fyfe, and it was as good as he'd imagined.

Fyfe's lips were soft but firm, and he didn't hesitate. He clearly knew what he wanted from James, and he prodded at his lips with his tongue until James opened. James knew he could back out of this any time he wanted, but he wasn't going to. He liked that Fyfe was kind of forceful. He liked that he could tell how much Fyfe wanted this and that he wasn't ashamed of it, that he wasn't going to be shy about it.

They were both a little breathless by the time Fyfe pressed one last kiss against James' lips and rested their foreheads together. "As much as I want to do this for the rest of the day and possibly the entire night, too, we need to go. I can feel the sun coming up, and I really need to get you to safety before the day starts."

"Where am I going?"

Fyfe got up and offered James his hand. James took it and leaned close to Fyfe, needing the comfort and the strength that emanated from Fyfe's body. He'd always made it on his own, but maybe now he wouldn't have to. It all depended on what was going to happen with the conclave, and for the first time, James decided he was going to do something about it. He wasn't sure what, so he was going to listen to Fyfe, but he was done fleeing and being hunted.

"I'll tell you once we're on our way. Come on. Let's go pack your stuff."

It didn't take long to do that. Even with the clothes and toiletries Fyfe had bought for James, everything still fit into James' backpack. He looked around Fyfe's bedroom before leaving. He was going to miss that room, even though he'd spent too much time in it. Most of all, he was going to miss Fyfe's presence in the bed with him, waking up with him and seeing him with his hair all over the place and the mark of his pillow on his cheek, all warm and soft with sleep.

Fyfe was never far as they left the house. They took Fyfe's car—a ridiculously small red sporty thing—and Fyfe drove too fast. James didn't say anything about it, not when he could see the first rays of the sun on the horizon. "How are you going to go home?"

"I won't, not this morning." Fyfe grinned. "I *can* stay out, you know. I might be the coven leader, but that doesn't mean I owe the coven my entire life. It won't be the first time I don't get home to sleep."

That made James jealous, but he wasn't stupid enough to think Fyfe had never had a lover. He was four hundred years old, for fuck's sake. "Are you going to tell me where we're going now?"

Fyfe drove like he did everything else. His hands were sure and secure on the wheel, and he didn't look away from the road, not even when he answered. "To a friend's. He's a vampire, but he doesn't want to be part of the coven. He lives with a human."

"They're together?"

"Yes."

"How does that work?"

Fyfe's lips quirked and he arched a brow. "Do I really have to explain that to you? It's been a while since I last had the birds and the bees conversation. Or was it the bees and flowers? I mean, it would make more sense."

James rolled his eyes. "You know what I mean. If your friend is a vampire and his partner is human, how are they going to make it work long-term?"

"Percy hopes Roan will agree to be bitten sooner or later, but they're not in a rush. Besides, the same could be said for us, couldn't it? You're a werewolf, but you're not immortal, not the way I am. How are we going to make it work?"

It wasn't the first time James thought about that, but he was already worried about surviving the next few weeks. "We'll talk about it later."

"Once you're safe from the conclave, yes."

Fyfe knew he was taking a risk by taking James to Percy's

apartment. He'd called Percy to ask first, of course, but he hadn't told him everything. He'd informed his friend that James was being hunted by the conclave for something he hadn't done, but that was it. He didn't think Percy wouldn't want to help if he found out the rest, but he couldn't risk it, not right now.

"So this is a friend of yours, right?" James asked as they walked out of the elevator in Percy's building."

"Yes."

"And he's a vampire."

"With a human boyfriend, yes. You'll like them."

James grimaced. "But will they like me? I mean, I *am* being hunted for murder."

Fyfe bit his lower lip. "They don't know that."

James stopped walking and glared at Fyfe. "You haven't told them?"

"I didn't have the time. I told them the conclave was after you and that you were innocent, and that's true."

"It is, but they should know what they're getting themselves into anyway."

Fyfe sighed. "I know. I just didn't have the time to go into lengthy explanations. I couldn't risk Percy saying no. But now that we're here, you'll be able to tell them yourself."

"What if they don't believe me?"

That was what Fyfe was afraid of. "Then I'll find another place for you. Don't worry, James. I'm not letting the conclave get to you." Fyfe knew James well enough to be aware he was going to thank him again for helping him, and he didn't want that. James had no reason to thank him, not when he was doing this for an entirely selfish reason.

He rushed toward the door to Percy's apartment without giving James time to talk and knocked on the door. Percy and Roan were expecting them, and the door opened only seconds after he'd knocked. Percy waved Fyfe and James inside, and Fyfe's heart warmed. He hadn't realized he and Percy were friends until Percy had called him for help. He was so busy with the coven that he didn't have much time for anyone else, but he needed to make it somehow, because Percy was doing him a huge favor.

Roan grinned when he saw Fyfe. "Hey there."

Fyfe couldn't help but smile back. Roan had that effect on him, and just about everyone else. "I'm sorry to bother you."

"You're not a bother. You're a friend." Roan peeked around Fyfe. "This is James?"

Fyfe introduced James to Percy and Roan. He expected Percy to ask what was going on even though he'd already explained. He was surprised when *James* was the one to bring it up, though, and he wished he could slap a hand on James' delicious lips.

"The conclave wants me because I've been accused of killing my alpha," James said as soon as Fyfe was done with the introductions.

Roan blinked at him. Percy arched a brow and asked, "And did you do it?"

"No. The beta did it. I'll understand if you were uncomfortable with having me here, though."

"We're not."

James looked up so fast that Fyfe was surprised his neck didn't crack. "You're not? But I just told you—"

"That you were accused of killing someone. Fyfe trusts you, though, and he clearly believes you, and that's enough for Roan and me. we don't need an explanation or proof that you're telling the truth."

"I . . . thank you, but that's not all. I'm a werewolf, and I haven't learned control yet. I *have* to shift when the moon is full, and when I do, I don't control the wolf. I've also shifted during the day a few times when I was especially angry. I'm dangerous."

"The full moon is still a few days away, right?"

"It is."

"Then you're welcome to stay. We can talk tomorrow about what you'll need for the full moon. I'm sure you're both tired. Fyfe, you know where the guest room is. We'll see you tomorrow."

Percy grabbed Roan on his way to bed. Fyfe watched them leave, his heart aching to have that same love and closeness. He'd been surprised when Percy had told him about Roan, especially after he'd lost his previous human lover to old age. They were happy, though, and Roan wasn't opposed to being bitten, so Fyfe hoped they'd have hundreds of years together.

"That was easier than I expected," James said.

"I told you they wouldn't care."

"Yeah, you did." James' voice was soft, and he sounded tired, so Fyfe took his hand and guided him to the guest room.

He hadn't spent many nights there, but he remembered where it was. He smiled when he saw someone—no doubt Roan—had left fresh towels on the dresser in the bedroom. The bathroom was tiny, but it was private, and it would be enough for James. Fyfe wished he could stay with him, but the coven needed him, and he wanted to be able to keep an eye on Alfred, just in case. He was probably reacting too harshly to Alfred's words, but he couldn't risk James.

"This is it," Fyfe said as he closed the door behind James.

James looked around. "It's nice."

"You won't have to stay long. I promise you, you'll be back home with me in a few weeks tops." Fyfe had had enough of waiting, and he was going to shake things up. He'd call Maurice and Ignatius again and see what was happening. James didn't deserve to have his life suspended for so long.

"Home?" James asked. There was something peculiar in his voice, like awe and sadness at the same time.

"Are you okay?"

"Yeah. It's just that I haven't had a home in a while. You make it sound like I belong."

Fyfe had never been great with feelings, but he'd learned things the hard way over the years. Talking was always what worked best. "The coven will be your home for as long as you want it to, and me too, if you want me."

The corner of James' lips curled up. "I thought I'd made that obvious."

"We kissed, and you've stuck around, but I can't read your mind, and we haven't talked about us. I understand you've had other, more important things in mind, but—"

"Yes."

Fyfe blinked. "Yes?"

"I want you and the coven to be my home once this is over." James frowned. "If it ends the right way."

Fyfe hated listening to James talk this way. He understood it, but he wished they didn't have to worry about whether James would be alive so they could have a future together.

He took James' hand and squeezed. "It will."

"You can't promise that."

"No, but I *can* promise I'll do whatever I have to do to make it happen."

"I know you will. I don't know what I did to deserve you, but—"

Fyfe pulled James into his arms and pressed their lips together. "You're you. That's enough to deserve the world." He kissed James again.

He wanted so much more than stolen kisses and nights spent sleeping in the same bed. He wanted James in his life for real, and forever. "Ready to go to bed?" he asked.

James nodded, and Fyfe let go of him. He couldn't look away as James took his clothes off. He usually kept on his boxer briefs and his t-shirt, but this time, he took his t-shirt off, then, looking at Fyfe, he also pushed his boxers down his legs.

Fyfe's mouth was suddenly dry. He licked his lips and didn't bother trying to hide that he was staring. James knew he was. He'd no doubt gotten naked on purpose. "James?" Fyfe croaked.

James' legs were hairy and strong, the thighs thick with muscles. His cock was half-hard already, and it hung between his legs, heavy-looking and surrounded by dark hair. Fyfe's mouth watered. He wanted to taste James, to learn him and to never forget him.

James' buttocks flexed as he moved toward the bed. He settled down under the blanket and looked at Fyfe, who was still wearing his jacket and couldn't bring himself to care about it. "Are you coming to bed?"

Fyfe swallowed. "Are you sure you want this?"

James rolled his eyes. "Don't you think I've thought of this plenty of times since I met you? I wanted to fuck you that first day in the warehouse, you know?"

"You . . . did?"

"Yeah. I didn't know you, and I didn't trust you, but I wanted you. And now that I know you, I want you even more. I thought waiting would be best because I might, well, you know, not be here for long, but I want this. I want to have something good to remember if the conclave decides I need to die."

The situation broke Fyfe's heart. No matter how many times he promised James he'd be safe, they both knew it was out of Fyfe's control. No matter how many people he knew and begged for favors, he didn't control the conclave. They'd do what they wanted, and he didn't have a say in it.

His heart would break if the conclave decided to execute James, and it would be worse if he let himself have this—if he allowed James in. But most of the damage was already done. Fyfe was falling in love with James, and nothing he did could stop that. Sleeping with him—having sex with him—certainly wouldn't, and if the memories they'd create helped James when he needed it, then Fyfe would do it.

He dropped his jacket on the floor and walked to the bed.

Chapter Five

James pushed his eggs around the plate and stared at them harder as if he could make them disappear. It wasn't that he *had* to eat them if he didn't want to, but this was Percy and Roan's food, and they were already doing so much for James that he didn't want to waste it.

The sound of a door and footsteps made James look up. Roan stumbled into the kitchen, still buttoning his shirt. He waved at James and almost tripped on his own feet on his way to the coffee machine. "You got a pot ready," he said, sounding delighted.

"Of course I did. And your phone and your keys are on the coffee table in the living room."

Roan turned, his hands wrapped around a steaming mug, and peered at James. "You're really bored, aren't you?"

James shrugged. He *was* bored, but it wasn't like he had a choice. He couldn't leave the apartment in case someone noticed him, just like he'd barely left Fyfe's room when he'd lived with the coven. He was starting to hate closed places, and his wolf longed to get some fresh air. That would happen soon enough, since the full moon was next week, but in the meantime, James was stuck.

"You didn't have to do all this," Roan said.

"I knew you'd be late, and I didn't want you to fret." He'd been with Percy and Roan for a few days, and Roan had gotten up late every morning. James supposed it was hard to still have a human day job while living with a vampire who was awake during the night. If Roan wanted to spend time with Percy, he had to stay up late, and he ended up getting up late, too.

Roan's smile was warm. "Well, thank you. I know you don't like it here, but I'm grateful I met you." His smile widened. "And not only because thanks to you I don't waste half an hour looking for my phone every morning."

James cleared his throat. "There's also a sandwich for your breakfast in the fridge."

"Really? Okay, don't tell Percy, but I think I love you."

James barked out a laugh. "Thanks, but you're not my type."

Roan wiggled his eyebrows. "You're more of a long, dark hair type, huh?"

"I don't know what you're talking about." And James was *not* going to blush. No one cared that he and Fyfe were together, especially not Percy and Roan.

"Sure you don't. Well, thanks for the coffee and everything else. I should go before I waste all your efforts and end up late."

James felt better after the short conversation with Roan. It was true that he was stuck in the apartment and that he spent his days alone since Percy slept, but things could be worse.

Since he didn't have anything else to do, he spent part of the morning cleaning the place. There wasn't much mess, but Roan tended to leave stuff around, and James had had enough of soap operas on TV, so cleaning was better than looking at the walls, or worse, out the window.

The knock that came mid-morning startled James. He wasn't expecting anyone—and since the only person who visited him was Fyfe, he'd have come during the night anyway—and Percy would have told him if *he* did. Who was it, then?

James doubted the conclave would knock on the door if it

was them. They'd knock it down and barge in to arrest his ass. "Who is it?" he called out.

"Richie."

The voice was male, and James didn't recognize it. He also didn't know a Richie. "Are you here for Percy?"

"Nope. You should call your boyfriend. I thought he was supposed to tell you I was coming?"

James blinked. He hadn't yet checked his phone, since Fyfe had spent most of the night with him, but sure enough, there was a text now that said that Richie would visit him this morning—and other things that James ignored until he could get Fyfe naked and in the bedroom. That man could have a filthy mouth and thoughts when he wanted to, no doubt thanks to the hundreds of years he'd spent thinking of sex and having it.

James opened the door.

He had no idea who Richie was or why he was there, but for some reason, he hadn't expected him to be, well, him.

Richie was short, maybe around five foot six. The fact that he was slight made him look even younger, but Fyfe wouldn't have sent him if he couldn't somehow help James. Besides, James doubted Richie was human. He wasn't a vampire, because he wouldn't be there in the morning if he were, but vampires weren't the only species who lived long lives. Werewolves weren't immortal like vamps, but they had long lives, and they aged very slowly. Richie could be eighty for all James knew.

And he was tattooed. It seemed like every inch of exposed skin was colored and signed, and James was curious about the designs. He didn't ask, though. Instead, he said, "Yes?"

Richie looked him up and down then pushed past him and walked into the apartment. "So you're the guy who made Fyfe go crazy?"

James closed the door and crossed his arms over his chest.

"I'm sorry?"

"You know. He's never asked me for a favor, not for someone else anyway. You're banging him?"

James gaped. "Why are you here?"

"Oh, he wants me to teach you control."

James blinked. "You're a werewolf."

"Gold star for you, pup."

"Don't call me that." James didn't mind when Fyfe called him pup too much, but he was the only one he'd allow to do that."

Richie shrugged and looked around. "Sure. This place smells of vamps."

"That's because it's not my apartment. You can teach me control?"

James would have been skeptical, but again, he didn't know how old Richie was. Everything was possible.

"Of course I can. I wouldn't be here otherwise."

"Why are you helping me, though?"

Richie toed his tennis shoes off and abandoned them by the door. His socks had little Santas printed on them. "Because Fyfe asked."

"And you do everything Fyfe asks?"

"Of course not." Richie folded legs and sat on the rug. He gestured at the spot in front of him in a clear invitation. James could have done without sitting on the floor, but he obeyed. He was the student in this case, even though Richie looked younger than him.

"Why are you helping me, then?"

Richie arched a blond brow. "You want to know what my relationship with Fyfe is." He grinned. "Don't worry. I'm over the crush I had on him. You can't blame me for wanting to fuck him, though. He's a gorgeous man, and more importantly, he's a *nice* man. He saved my ass a few decades ago. Nothing I can do will ever repay him for that, so any time he needs me, I'll come. Are you ready to start?"

James wasn't afraid of Fyfe cheating on him, with Richie or with anyone else. He *was* curious about the past Fyfe shared with Richie, but Richie didn't look like he was going to tell him, and that was okay. James hoped he'd have decades to get to know Fyfe and his friends, including Richie.

But he'd have a chance at that only if he learned control — and if the conclave got their heads out of their asses. He couldn't do anything about *that*, but he could learn how to control his wolf and how not to be a danger to people. "Yes."

"All right. It's simple, really. Have you ever tried to meditate?"

"No."

"You need to be calm, so close your eyes and breathe."

Considering James hated staying still and silent, it was easier said than done, but then he'd known learning control wouldn't be easy. He'd tried before, and it hadn't gone well. Still, he closed his eyes and breathed in and out, centering himself and trying to ignore the fact that he could feel Richie watching him

"Good." Richie's voice was soft. It barely intruded in James' focus. "Now reach out to your wolf. You have to find the corner of your mind where he's hiding. The fact that you don't have control means he doesn't trust you to have it. That can happen when a human is recently bitten. He just wants to keep you safe."

James could do without that, but there was no separating him and his wolf. There'd never be. Lycanthropy wasn't something one healed from, and he had to learn to live with it.

Fyfe wanted to see James, damn it. He was staying away tonight because he knew Richie was probably still with James and that James didn't need to be distracted, but still. He missed his man.

He wasn't sure what to call him. His boyfriend? He hadn't called anyone boyfriend in years. Besides, James felt more important, like a partner. That particular word reminded Fyfe of partners in crime, though. He and James could certainly be considered that, but it didn't describe their relationship. Lover, maybe? That was the one Fyfe preferred, but younger people would probably laugh at him for using it because it sounded old.

It didn't matter. Fyfe *was* old.

The door of his office burst open, shattering his daydreaming. Aubrey barged in, his eyes wide, his face paler than usual. "Fyfe?"

Fyfe was already up. "What's wrong?"

"The conclave? They're here. The enforcers."

"Here? Where?"

"At the door. I tried to stop them from coming in, but—"

"But they did anyway." Fyfe wasn't surprised the conclave had authority over him and his coven. Still, they should have asked to talk to him before forcing their way in. "Don't worry about it."

"It's my job to—"

"It's your job to protect the coven, and you do it well. You don't have to protect us from the conclave." That would be suicide, and Fyfe didn't want to lose anyone.

He left the office, Aubrey trailing behind him. He wasn't surprised to find the front door open and the entrance full of conclave enforcers. They all wore the black uniform with the red logo on the breast, and most of them looked like they were ready to tear apart anyone who tried to stop them.

"To what do I owe this pleasure?" Fyfe drawled as he walked down the stairs.

The man closest to the stairs looked up at him. "I'm Oren."

"I'm Fyfe, this coven's leader. Why did you barge in without even waiting for me to arrive?"

"We were told you're harboring a criminal."

Fyfe had expected this. He was still disappointed. "Oh? And who told you that?"

Oren's eyes flickered to the corner of the room. Fyfe wasn't surprised to see Alfred huddled there, along with another two elders. He sighed. "Of course. Well, I can assure you I'm doing nothing of the sort."

"They're together," Alfred spat out.

"It's certainly true that I have a werewolf lover, but he's not a criminal. Besides, he left a few days ago."

Alfred's eyes widened, but he didn't say anything. All he knew was James' name, and while Fyfe found James incredibly beautiful, he wasn't uncommon looking. Even if Alfred could identify him from a picture — and Fyfe doubted it since James had spent most of his time with the coven in Fyfe's bedroom — he had no way to prove James *was* the werewolf the conclave was looking for. "You won't object to us searching the coven, then?"

Fyfe wanted to, but he knew how to pick his battles, and a big one was coming, because as soon as the conclave enforcers left, he was kicking Alfred's ass out of the coven. "Of course not. I only ask that you knock on the doors of the private bedrooms before you enter, and of course, that you limit yourself to looking for this criminal you told me about. I won't have you search my family's private papers or anything of the sort."

Oren straightened his back. "Of course not. We're acting on the conclave's orders. We aren't robbers or common criminals."

Fyfe wanted to say he'd met his fair share of enforcers

who thought themselves above the law and common decency, but he didn't. He needed Oren and his people to do their job and leave. They wouldn't find anything—Fyfe had made sure James hadn't left anything behind, and he'd changed his sheets and done the laundry, so they wouldn't be able to smell him, either.

Fyfe walked Oren to his bedroom himself. He opened the door with a flourish, and Oren walked in after looking at him for a touch too long. Fyfe cleared his throat. "So, this criminal you're looking for, what has he done?"

"He killed his alpha. You said you have a werewolf lover?"

"Ah, yes. I have to admit I'm not surprised Alfred tried to get rid of him this way. He's old school, you know. He doesn't like vampires mixing with other species, but especially not with werewolves. He tried to convince me to break up with my man, but I told him to take a hike. He obviously thought he'd have more luck this way."

"But your lover already left."

"Yes. He didn't think it smart to spend the full moon here, not when I haven't yet prepped a room for him yet."

"And the coven members don't mind having him around? Apart from Alfred, of course," Oren asked as he opened the bathroom door.

"Most of them are younger than Alfred. Besides, you know the coven is accepting of vampires who have been rejected by their own coven or makers for various reasons."

"They're all vampires, though."

"I know. It's only because I haven't had the occasion to welcome anyone else into the coven. I'm not opposed to having different species living with us. I don't believe in entire species being bad, or whatever Alfred thinks. All supernatural species have bad and good people. I don't mind the good ones."

"I see."

"Do you?" Fyfe didn't know Oren, hadn't even heard of him, but he *did* know Ignatius. His friend wanted to change the world, and he wouldn't agree to work under a man who didn't see things the way he did.

Oren was done looking around, and he came back to the door. "I do. As you might have noticed, I don't only lead vampires. Some members of my team are werewolves, witches, or other supernatural beings."

Fyfe nodded. "I know. One of my oldest friends works with you. Ignatius."

Oren arched a brow. "You wouldn't happen to have something to do with the reason he went back to the pack to talk to the beta?"

"I don't know what you're talking about." Fyfe was pretty sure he wasn't fooling Oren, but as long as Oren didn't insist, he would be fine.

"I see. Well, everything looks good here."

Fyfe led him to several other rooms. When he was done, he and his team met in the entrance again, and Oren glared at Alfred, who hadn't left his spot next to the door. He looked smaller, as if the righteousness had fled him once he'd realized James really was gone.

Oren looked around, but all his team members shook their heads. Fyfe didn't relax yet, though. He'd allow that only once the enforcers had left.

"I'm sorry we interrupted your night," Oren said.

"You were doing your job. You couldn't have known the person who contacted you was lying."

"I hope you'll take care of that."

Fyfe smiled. "Don't worry. I will." And he was looking forward to it.

Aubrey and the other guards went with the enforcers to make sure they left, and Fyfe turned to Alfred. "You. In my office, right now. The same goes for anyone who thinks you did the right thing by calling the conclave."

Fyfe wasn't surprised when Alfred was the only one who followed him. He knew other elders thought the way he did, but none of them wanted to get kicked out. A vampire without a coven was vulnerable. The coven took care of always having blood bags and making sure all its members fed well. The guards kept the coven safe, and the house they lived in was comfortable, some would even say luxurious. Alfred would have nothing of that now, and he knew it. Fyfe felt a little guilty, but he couldn't allow the betrayal. Coven members should be loyal to the coven and their leader.

Alfred hadn't been.

Fyfe was going to have to talk to Alfred's friends and make sure they understood they'd share Alfred's fate if they went against Fyfe. He didn't like it, but it was part of being the leader. They were lucky he wasn't like their old leader, who hadn't had a problem beating or whipping them, or even killing them.

Alfred didn't protest when Fyfe told him to leave. He had his dignity, Fyfe supposed. "I want you out of here in two hours at most. You are not welcome here anymore, Alfred. And I'm sorry for that."

Alfred tried to look defiant, but Fyfe thought he appeared sad more than anything. "I did the right thing. You'll ruin the coven."

"Be that as it may, the solution wasn't to betray me. I'm sorry you couldn't open your mind up enough to realize there's nothing wrong with most werewolves. Goodbye, Alfred." Fyfe hoped he wouldn't see him again because he knew that if he did, it would be because Alfred was creating problems for him again.

James was glad for the ring of his phone. He'd been working with Richie for most of the day, then again for part of the night, and he needed a break, even if it was a short one. "I have to answer this."

Richie rolled his eyes, and Roan snickered. "Of course you do."

James wasn't sure why Roan found watching him learn control so interesting, but he'd stuck to the living room since he'd come back from work. Percy was in the kitchen, cooking for the three of them—James had been surprised to find out he was a good cook since he didn't eat food—and making James feel guilty for that.

It was Fyfe, and James smiled as he answered. "Hey. Are you coming over tonight?"

Fyfe sighed. "I don't think that's wise. I don't want you to freak out, but the conclave enforcers were here today. Alfred called them and told them you were here with the coven."

Fyfe had warned James, yet it didn't stop him from doing precisely what Fyfe had told him not to do—he freaked out. "Do they know I'm here with Percy and Roan? I need to leave. I don't want anyone to get hurt over me."

"You need to stay where you are, James. Running away isn't going to help."

"What if they find me? What's going to happen to Percy?"

"They won't find you. Alfred is gone, and even if he were still here, he doesn't know we're friends."

"He can find out."

A hand landed on James' back. He jerked, but it was only Richie, who mouthed, "Breathe."

James wanted to tell him to fuck off. How was he supposed to breathe when his friends were in danger because of him? But Richie glared, and James found himself obeying.

He relaxed and took the time to calm down. Fyfe and Richie were right. Freaking out and acting on instinct and fear wasn't going to help. "Are you okay?" he asked once he could think clearly again.

"Yes. Everyone is. Well, except Alfred, but that's his own fault. I wouldn't have told him to leave if he hadn't forced me to by betraying me and the coven. But the leader of the enforcers' team the conclave sent seems like a nice guy, and I know Ignatius wouldn't work with him if he weren't. I'm not sure why he's after you, to be honest. There has to be someone higher up who's pulling the strings."

Knowing that one of the men who wanted to kill him wasn't eager about it didn't make James feel better, but maybe it would help. "You're sure everyone is all right?"

"Yes, I am. And I wish I could come over tonight, but the coven needs me. I want to talk to them and explain what happened with Alfred. They probably already know, but just in case, I want to reassure them and remind them of the rules I decided on when I agreed to become their leader."

"And you're sure I shouldn't leave? Maybe find another place to hide?"

"No. Stay with Percy and Roan, please. I know it's asking a lot, but I promise I'm doing everything I can. I'm going to call Ignatius again and see what he found out. His team leader, Oren, knows he's back with the pack and that he's investigating. I think that's why he didn't push more after Alfred's allegations. He knows I have a werewolf boyfriend, yet he didn't even ask me your name. He has to know you really were here, but he's closing an eye. I'll also call my friend in the conclave and find out who's behind this. Someone wants you to pay for this whether you did it or not."

"I didn't."

"I know. How are things going with Richie?"

James eyed Richie and decided to go talk on the balcony. Richie stuck his tongue out when he noticed, then turned to Roan. Those two seemed to get on like a house on fire, so

James wasn't worried.

He slid the balcony door shut behind him and looked at the sky. He wanted to be with Fyfe right now, to make sure he really was safe like he was saying he was. He had to trust him, though. They both had to trust each other, or they wouldn't work, not with everything they had against them.

"James'" Fyfe asked.

"Sorry. I needed some privacy. Richie is still here."

"He is? Wait, let me guess. He and Roan are already friends."

"How did you know?"

"I know both of them well enough." James was pretty sure Fyfe was smiling. He could hear it in his voice.

"Yeah, they're getting on well. Richie's one of a kind, isn't he?"

"He is."

"How did you meet him?"

"You haven't asked him?"

"Of course I have. He just said you saved his life."

"I did. He'll tell you more if he wants you to know, though. I'd been trying to call him ever since I met you, but he was out of town. He only came back yesterday. Is he helping you?"

"Kind of? I mean, he's trying, but I've never been good with meditation and whatnot."

"You'll manage. All werewolves do."

Because if they didn't, the conclave or their pack took care of them. Fyfe didn't need to say it for James to know it. "I will. I just need to work on it." James hoped he'd be able to stay in control during the full moon, but he knew that was the worst time of the month to try. It was when the wolf was strongest and when he didn't have a choice whether he wanted to shift or not. But if he could do this, if he could keep control, then the rest of the month would be a walk in the park.

"I believe in you, pup. You can do this."

That warmed James' heart more than anything else could. He didn't have anyone in his life anymore. He'd left his family behind when he'd been bitten because he hadn't wanted to hurt them or to have to watch them look at him with fear and disgust. The pack had taken him in, but most of its members had never warmed up to him. The only new wolves there had been the ones who'd been born that way, like Oscar, and they hadn't wanted a newly bitten wolf like James with them.

Then he'd met Fyfe.

Fyfe hadn't had a reason to trust James or to help him, but he had. He'd brought him home and had protected him. He was still protecting him, and he was doing all he could to make sure James made it out of this situation, that he had a choice and a future. James would never be able to repay him for everything he'd done, but he intended to try. If he was ever recognized as innocent, he'd stay around for as long as Fyfe wanted him. He didn't know how long that would be, but it didn't matter. Fyfe deserved everything he wanted, and everything James could give him.

And that included him learning to control his wolf.

"You know I'd like nothing more than talking to you all night," he told Fyfe.

"Same here, but we both have things to do."

"We do. I wish I could be there with you, though."

"You will soon enough. Don't worry about me. I'm fine, and I will continue to be. Work with your wolf, and when the moon is full, we'll spend the night together. I've always wanted to pet a werewolf."

James chuckled. "You'll be able to." He could feel the wolf in the back of his mind, and he knew it didn't mind. It liked Fyfe. James wasn't sure how that worked—was the wolf half in love with Fyfe like James was, or did he just like him? There was so much James didn't know about were-wolves, things he'd never been told. Maybe Richie could help him with that, too.

"Get to work, my little king," Fyfe said, hanging up before James could protest.

James wasn't sure he liked the nicknames, be it pup or king. Where had that one come from anyway?

"Everything okay?" Richie asked when James went back to the living room.

"The conclave was at the house."

"Those assholes. Does Fyfe need me to kick some ass?"

James *really* liked Richie. "He told me to stay put, so I don't think so. He's taking care of everything, whatever that means."

"I wouldn't worry, then. Fyfe has a way of making things work out."

James hoped Richie would be proven right. He was ready to start this new part of his life.

Fyfe wanted to run to Percy's apartment, but he stayed right where he was. James was busy, and even if he weren't, Fyfe couldn't afford someone following him. He had no way of knowing whether Oren had believed him, or if he and his team were waiting outside the house.

Well, that wasn't exactly true. He *did* have a way to find out, but his way was with James' old pack right now, or at least he should be. Fyfe hadn't heard from Ignatius since he'd first called him, and he didn't want to disturb him, but he wouldn't mind an update.

He called. He'd never been one to have patience, not when it wasn't necessary. If Ignatius couldn't answer for whatever reason, then he wouldn't. He wasn't a pushover.

"What do you want now?" Ignatius snapped.

Fyfe grinned. "To hear the sweet sound of your voice."

"I'm not in the mood, Fyfe. Has something happened?"

"Don't you keep in touch with your team?"

"Mostly. I don't get a minute by minute replay, though."

Fyfe reclined on his bed. "Well, I got a visit from your team. Oren is a splendid specimen."

"And he's not an animal. Also, I have to work with him every day, so can you please stop talking about him that way?"

"You used to be more fun."

"I used to think people were mostly decent."

"Oh, Igni. I thought the centuries had healed you of that."

"They did. I've seen too much to still think that way since I started working for the conclave."

Fyfe grimaced. He didn't like hearing his friend talking that way, but there was nothing he could do. "It's that bad? You're with James' pack, right?"

Ignatius sighed. "Yeah, I am, and yeah, it is. They're assholes, Fyfe, and I'm not even talking about what they did to James."

The fact that it sounded like Ignatius believed what Fyfe had said about James made Fyfe feel better, but what he believed didn't mean that he had found proof of James' innocence. "What's going on? If you can talk about it, of course, but you know I won't tell anyone."

"Not even James?"

"I'm pretty sure he knows what's happening in that place."

"Yeah. He's the one who told you about Oscar?"

"He did. He said Oscar was the one who freed him. Is he okay?" It was too easy to imagine Oscar had been punished for what he'd done, and Fyfe didn't want to think about what that punishment had been. It was true he didn't hate werewolves, but he couldn't deny a lot of them were more aggressive and bloodthirsty than anyone else he'd ever met. It was a part of having to share their body with a wolf, but it could lead to unpleasant things, especially for the weaker members of packs.

"He was whipped, but he's in good condition."

Fyfe closed his eyes. He'd been whipped a few times in the past, and he could still feel the sting of every lash on his back. Much depended on who was doing the whipping and how they felt while they were doing it, of course, and Fyfe hoped that whoever had hurt Oscar hadn't been too angry. "Good condition?"

"I'm, ah, waiting for him to be able to travel to come back."

That wasn't something Fyfe had expected. He wasn't sure what question to start with. "You said he was in good condition, but he can't travel yet. James has been on the run for several weeks. That's not what I call good condition, Ignatius."

"He wasn't found right away, and the pack took a while to decide what to do with him considering he's the son of the new alpha."

Fyfe could accept that. "But why are you waiting for him to be able to travel? He's coming here with you?"

There was a moment of silence, and Fyfe *knew* Ignatius was hiding something. He wanted to prod, but he knew his friend would tell him if he wanted to, or if he needed to. "Yes, he's coming back with me."

"I see." Fyfe wasn't seeing anything because that wasn't an explanation. "Can I ask why?"

"For fuck's sake, Fyfe. You really have to stick your nose into everything?"

Fyfe was slightly offended by that. "I don't, but this situation is important to me."

"Because you like James."

"I'll be honest with you if you are honest with me."

"And let me guess, you want me to start."

Fyfe chuckled. "You know me so well." And Ignatius didn't have as much to lose as Fyfe and James did.

"This pack is isolationist. They stick to the forest, and they don't normally accept members who were bitten. All of the families here have been born wolves for centuries. They think they're keeping the blood pure by doing this."

Fyfe snorted. "Really? Don't they know there's no difference between a born wolf and a bitten one?"

"I'm pretty sure they do, but I don't claim to understand the way they think. That said, I'm still not sure why the alpha thought taking James in was a good idea. I'm not surprised your friend was ostracized by most of the other wolves."

"Most, but not all." Fyfe could read between the lines when he needed to.

"Not all," Ignatius confirmed.

It wasn't hard to guess where he was going. "Let me guess—Oscar is one of the few wolves who liked James and didn't care how his wolf came to be."

"Exactly. I haven't been able to talk to him much because I'm forbidden from going anywhere near him, but I snuck into his room. He and James became friends, kind of. They weren't allowed to spend time together, but Oscar is sweet and lonely. He also wants to do what's right, even though he doesn't have any kind of power here."

Now Fyfe got it. "You want to protect him."

"It's not a bad thing," Ignatius snapped.

"I never said it was. It's *not*. If you think Oscar needs to leave his pack, then you should help him to leave. I can welcome him into the coven. Both him and you, of course." Fyfe wasn't sure Ignatius would accept that offer, but he meant it.

Ignatius wanted to do good things, and he'd clearly thought working for the conclave was the way to do it. It meant he wouldn't be able to protect Oscar, though, and Fyfe doubted Oscar's pack would let him leave. He'd be protected if he became a coven member, even if Ignatius had to leave.

"Why would you do that?" Ignatius' voice was strangled.

"Why not? Oscar obviously needs help, and if you trust him, I trust him, too."

"He's a werewolf."

"He won't be the only werewolf coven member, not if I have a say about it. Although of course, that depends on whether or not you can prove James didn't do anything."

"I *knew* there was more to this than just knowing that guy."

Fyfe rolled his eyes. "Of course you did. I'm not exactly discreet when I like someone."

"Is he there with you, Fyfe?" Ignatius was more serious now, and Fyfe knew he was worried.

"He's not. Your team came around today. One of the elders called them and told them I was harboring a criminal. They didn't find anyone, of course."

"Of course. Be careful, Fyfe. Please."

"Always. And my offer stands, for both you and Oscar. I didn't have a choice in becoming the leader of this coven, but I can put that to good use. I've been wary of the elders for too long, and look what happened."

"I hate that someone betrayed you. You don't deserve it."

"He won't betray me again, don't worry. I kicked his ass out as soon as Oren and the rest of your team left. And I'm done letting anyone else make decisions here."

"That's good to hear. And thanks for your offer. I think Oscar is going to need a new family once this is over. I'm not leaving him here, not when his own father whipped him and plans to sell him off."

That was news, but Fyfe wasn't surprised. He'd seen a lot of horrible things over the decades, and a lot of them had been perpetrated by parents or family in general. One couldn't choose blood family, unfortunately. "Bring him here, Igni. He has a place, and so do you. He'll never have to be afraid again." If Fyfe could only do one thing to thank Oscar for what he'd done, this was it.

Chapter Six

When the door slammed open, James knew this was it. He'd been found, and things weren't going to end well for him.

He stayed where he was on the couch and watched the conclave enforcers stream in. They were led by a big blond man who looked around and arched a brow when he spotted James. James tried to remember his name. He'd been told the first time he'd been arrested.

"James Beltran," the man said.

Oren—now he remembered. "The others don't know you're looking for me. I didn't tell them." James might not be able to get out of this, but he was going to do everything he could so that Percy and Roan didn't have to pay. They'd opened their home to him because they were Fyfe's friends. They didn't deserve to be in trouble because of that.

Oren stopped in front of James. "They don't know, huh?"

"No. I swear. I told them I needed a place to stay because my pack had kicked me out. Nothing more."

"We'll have to talk to them anyway."

"I realize that." And James hoped they'd stick with his story.

Oren nodded. "Get up."

James swallowed and obeyed. Nothing he could do or say would save him, and there would be no Oscar freeing him, not this time around. James wished he could have seen Fyfe one last time, but he was already lucky he'd met him and had been able to spend as much time as he had with him.

This was a good moment in his life for him to die—he'd known happiness and had started to fall in love with Fyfe, but they hadn't spent enough time together that Fyfe would mourn him for long. He'd be sad, and angry, but he'd get over it, and James would take the happiness to his grave.

Oren nodded at two of his enforcers. They grabbed James' arms and pulled him forward. They weren't nice about it, and James breathed in and out deeply. He couldn't allow the wolf to come out, but it was hard this close to the full moon. Thank God he'd worked with Richie long enough that he understood what he needed to do.

One particularly hard push made James almost fall to his knees. His wolf reared up, and James felt himself start to change. His nails elongated, and fur sprouted on the back of his hands. The wolf wanted to protect James and itself. It wanted to come out and fight, since James wouldn't do it. It wanted to tear apart the people threatening to kill them.

James wanted to give up control and let the wolf do it. He didn't want to die. He'd thought it would be easier than having to run for the rest of his life, but he'd met Fyfe, and that had changed everything. The enforcers wouldn't hesitate to kill him if he as much as growled at them, and James couldn't allow it. He didn't have much hope left, but the little he did have made him wait. If he had one chance to be with Fyfe, to live the rest of his life as a free man, then he wasn't going to ruin everything by tearing apart enforcers.

He let himself fall to his knees and close his eyes. He did his best to ignore what was going on around him—Roan's protests, Percy's quieter voice, the enforcers searching the house. He *needed* to rein the wolf in.

"Breathe in and out," a voice said.

James thought it was Oren, but could it really be? Why would the man care when having James shift would give him a chance to kill him right there and then? That was why he was there after all, wasn't it?

James gritted his teeth. A hand landed on the back of his neck, and he focused on the contact, on the fingers squeezing without creating pain, on how it anchored him into his human form. His wolf huffed and puffed and tried to push forward, but James pushed back. He understood why the wolf wanted to intervene, but this was the worst place and time.

"Good man. Continue to breathe," Oren said.

"Why are you doing this?" James said through his gritted teeth.

"Because I don't want to have to kill you."

James snorted. "That's why you're here, though."

"No. I'm here to arrest you because you're suspected of murder."

"Yet the last time we met, you were ready to kill me without investigating."

Oren didn't answer right away, but when he did, he stunned James. "I had different orders them. From a different member of the conclave."

James blinked. He hadn't expected so much candor from Oren. "You did?" This had Fyfe written all over it. He'd been working for James ever since they'd first met in the warehouse. James had known about it, but he hadn't believed Fyfe could actually make a difference.

But maybe he had. Maybe James wasn't going to get killed. Maybe he could let himself hope that someone was going to investigate what had happened. It would be the new alpha's word against his, but the enforcers weren't pack members. They might believe him. At the very least, they might look into it.

James took one last deep breath and pushed the wolf away with more strength. He had to promise he'd let it take over if it looked like they were going to be killed, but the wolf retreated, albeit grumpily. It still didn't trust James to do what was best for both of them, and James understood that.

When James opened his eyes, Oren was crouching next to him, looking at him. He nodded approvingly and got up. He didn't offer James his hand, but he stayed close, and when the two enforcers moved toward James again, he glared at them. "I said take him away, not push him around. We have new orders."

"But—" one of the enforcers started to say.

"But nothing. We have orders. *You* have orders, and they are to take him in without hurting him."

That was more than James had expected. He nodded in thanks at Oren, who didn't answer. Then he allowed himself to look around again.

Percy and Roan were huddled in a corner. Percy's arms were around Roan, who looked like he wanted to tell the enforcers to fuck off and maybe to fight them. James was glad Percy was holding him back. The fact that he was human wouldn't save him from the conclave, and attacking the enforcers was a sure way to be sentenced to death.

"I'll be okay," James said, hoping to calm Roan down.

Roan's eyes were blazing, though. "I sure hope you will, since you didn't do anything."

"Percy," James begged.

Percy nodded and held Roan tighter. James let the two enforcers from before lead him out. He didn't look back. He couldn't, not when he knew he was losing everything—Fyfe, Percy and Roan, the possibility of a new life. Everything wasn't done already, but even though he was hopeful again, James realized his chances were slim.

He let the enforcers push and pull him downstairs and into a van. He supposed he should be happy they hadn't blindfolded him or something. He wondered if Fyfe would be able to find out where they were taking James. He had no doubt Percy and Roan would call him as soon as they could and that he'd try to get to him.

James didn't know where the enforcers took him. The two who'd grabbed him were in front of the van, Oren in the back with him. Oren wasn't looking at him, but it didn't matter. James hadn't expected any kind of sympathy from the man. He hadn't gotten any the first time around, and even though things seemed to have changed, Fyfe couldn't work miracles.

James wasn't surprised to see a warehouse when the van stopped and he was pulled from it. It wasn't the one he'd hidden in that first night. It wasn't abandoned. It was a conclave building, as the discreet sign over the door proclaimed. There were people inside walking around and talking when James was led in. They didn't even turn to look at him. They were probably used to people being brought in by the enforcers.

The interrogation room was just a room. He was given a chair, and he could lean against the cold metal table and rest. He wasn't sure how much time he still had, but he didn't think it would be much, and he was obviously going to be interrogated before he got an answer to the most important question he had right now—was he going to be executed?

Fyfe's phone rang. He felt like he'd just hung up after his conversations with Ignatius first, and Maurice next. Still, it might be James, so he rolled over—he was conducting business from his bedroom today just because he could—and grabbed the phone from the pillow. He frowned when he saw Percy's name flashing on the screen. "Hello?"

"The enforcers came," Percy said.

Fyfe jerked up into a sitting position. "James?"

"They took him. Probably to some conclave building in town. I don't know. They didn't exactly stop to tell me. Roan and I are lucky they didn't arrest us, too." He sighed. "I'm sorry, Fyfe. I wish I could have done more, but I had to protect Roan."

Fyfe's heart was in his throat, and he was already looking for his shoes. "Don't worry about it. You did everything you could, and I'm grateful for your help."

"Let us know when you find out what's happening, okay? James grew on us, and Roan likes him."

"I will."

"And call us if you need anything. I can leave Roan home and come with you."

"The fuck you'll leave me home," Roan said in the background.

Fyfe smiled even though there was little to be happy about. "I hope I won't need your help, but thanks for offering."

Fyfe was only half surprised to find a small group of people waiting for him in the entrance. "What are you doing?" he asked Andrew, Falkner, and Aubrey.

"We're coming with you," Aubrey said.

"The conclave won't have it. You know this can't end well. And how did you find out about this anyway?" When it came to that, how had the conclave found out where James was?

Aubrey snorted. "You think you're the only one who knows Percy? He texted me as soon as he hung up with you. He doesn't want you to go alone, and I agree."

"You could be hurt or worse."

"We know."

Andrew and Falkner nodded. Fyfe was happy to see they were openly holding hands. He wanted them to stay home, though. If something happened to him, if the conclave decided he needed to die along with James, he didn't want his coven members to pay. They'd already have a hard enough time finding a new leader and dealing in the meantime.

But those three wouldn't be dissuaded, not easily, and Fyfe didn't have time to waste. They were adults, and they knew what they were doing. If they wanted to come, they could. "Let's go, then. Aubrey, you're driving." Fyfe needed to call Ignatius, and he didn't want them to be stopped because he was driving too fast.

"Twice in one night, Fyfe?" Ignatius asked when he answered.

"Your team arrested James."

"Fuck! Shit, I didn't think Oren knew where he was."

"I didn't either. I don't know how they found out, and right now, I don't care. I need to get to him and stop whatever they're doing, okay?" But Fyfe didn't know *where* James was. He wasn't part of the conclave. He knew there were several conclave buildings in town, but how was he supposed to know which one he needed to go to?

"They'll take him to the warehouse," Ignatius said, and Fyfe would have kissed him if they'd been together.

"Which warehouse?"

"I'll text you the address when we hang up. I'm not in town yet, but almost. I'm calling Oren as soon as we're done, but I need you to use up some time with them. I need an hour, more or less."

"I'll do my best." And Fyfe was ready to die trying. James didn't deserve to be killed for something he didn't do, and Fyfe was going to make sure it didn't happen.

"I'm sure you will."

Luckily for them, Aubrey knew where the warehouse was, and he drove them straight there. Fyfe had no idea if they'd be allowed in, but he was going to find out even if he had to fight. He knew that the penalty for attacking enforcers was more often than not death, but would that really matter if James was killed? He felt like a tragic hero even thinking that, but Fyfe *was* ready to die for James. A lot of people would think him stupid for that, but he'd learned to cherish every love he found over the hundreds of years he'd lived through. Besides, he'd have to die sooner or later. He couldn't say he was ready for it, but he'd face it if he had to.

Aubrey parked the car in front of the warehouse. It looked like every other warehouse Fyfe had seen, but he noticed the sign over the door.

"What now?" Falkner asked.

"Do we knock?" That was Andrew, who always tried to make people smile even in the direst of situations.

"That's a good idea." Fyfe hoped Ignatius was on the phone with Oren right now and that he and his friends wouldn't get killed on sight.

He strode to the door and knocked. He only had to wait a few seconds for it to open, and he didn't hesitate to push his way in. "What the fuck do you think you're doing?" the woman who'd opened growled.

Fyfe wasn't scared of her. "I want to see Oren, right now."

The woman looked like she wanted to tear Fyfe's head off with her bare hands. He wouldn't have been surprised if she could do it, either. "He's busy, and you have no business being here."

"I do when my lover has been taken in without a reason."

"Your *lover*?"

"I don't have time to waste. Either you go fetch Oren, or I will."

She crossed her arms over her chest. "You can try."

"I'll take care of her," Aubrey drawled behind Fyfe.

Fyfe was grateful, but she wasn't the only one around. Their conversation had caught the attention of the other people hanging around the entrance. The woman wasn't going to be the only one defending the place.

"You're sure?" Fyfe asked without looking at Aubrey. They both knew what they risked, and Fyfe didn't want Aubrey, Andrew, and Falkner to do this because they thought they owed him something. They didn't.

Aubrey patted Fyfe's shoulder. "Yep. Go get your man."

Fyfe wasn't going to ask again. He stepped aside, looking around and wondering where James would have been taken. If he wasn't being executed right now—and Fyfe fucking hoped he wasn't—he was probably being interrogated. And where would the interrogation rooms be? Fyfe was ready to bet it was where the enforcers watching had gathered. There were more of them to his left, standing in front of a set of double doors.

He headed that way.

He hadn't actually expected to make it there. He knew he wouldn't be able to get to James. The place was crawling with enforcers whose only job was to defend it. But maybe he could cause enough of a ruckus to give Ignatius the time he needed to arrive. Hopefully, he'd managed to talk to Oren so he knew something was happening.

He pushed his braid back and waited for the first enforcer. The man was as big as a bull, and like one, he charged Fyfe head on. This was the easiest kind of person to defeat because the enforcer only used his force, not his intelligence.

Fyfe moved to the side and let the guy pass. It didn't take him long to turn around, but Fyfe was already moving. He swung onto the bull's back and wrapped his arm around the man's neck. The man bucked, but Fyfe wasn't going anywhere. It felt a bit like riding a real bull, but he wasn't in the mood for having fun. He needed the guy to go down, and fast.

"What the fuck is going on here?" a voice boomed.

The guy Fyfe was sitting on froze. Fyfe didn't release him, but he looked up. Oren stood by the double doors Fyfe had noticed earlier. His arms were crossed over his chest, and he was glaring.

Aubrey had managed to knock the woman down and was now sitting astride a guy. Andrew's lower lip was bleeding, while Falkner was holding his arm close to his chest. All in all, it looked exactly like what it was—a fight.

Fyfe let go of the bull's back and hopped off. "Oren. You took James."

Oren arched a brow. "He's still accused of having killed his alpha."

"I know. How is he? Is he okay?" He didn't ask if he was still alive. He wasn't sure he could handle a negative answer right now.

"He is. Ignatius called me." Oren looked back at Aubrey and the others. "The four of you, come with me."

"Are we under arrest?" Falkner asked. "Because I think I need a doctor."

Oren rolled his eyes. "You're not. Let's go. James is waiting for you bunch of idiots."

Fyfe's heart skipped a beat. James was okay.

He was *okay*.

James knew it was Oren when the door opened again, but he hadn't expected Fyfe, Andrew, Falkner, and Aubrey to file in with him.

James got up so abruptly that his chair almost fell on the floor. He stared at Fyfe with wide eyes, trying to understand whether he'd been arrested for doing something foolish like trying to free James or if he was there to take James home. James couldn't tell, but when he moved toward Fyfe and Oren didn't say anything, he threw himself into Fyfe's waiting arms.

They closed around him.

He sighed, the tension and fear releasing the hold they had on his chest, at least for now. "What are you doing here?" he asked as he inhaled Fyfe's scent.

"Where else would I be, pup? I came as soon as Percy called me." Fyfe looked at Oren. "How did you find out that was where James was?"

Oren grimaced. "Another call from your coven."

"Dammit. I'm going to have to kick someone else out. Oh, well. I suppose it's just as well since it seems I'm about to get at least two new members."

James looked at Fyfe. "You are?"

Fyfe brushed James' cheekbone with a fingertip. "I think so, but I'll know more when Ignatius arrives."

Oren huffed. "How did you manage to get one of my best men to work against me?"

"He's not working against you. He's working for justice, no matter the result. He's always been like that."

"I see. You're old acquaintances."

"Isn't everyone in our world?"

"He called me."

Fyfe nodded. He pulled James back to his side of the table, and while James would have done pretty much anything to not sit in that chair again, he went. It was easier to sit there when Fyfe elegantly flopped into it and pulled James onto his lap. James' cheeks heated, but he snuggled against Fyfe's chest and tried to make the most of the moment. It might still be the last they'd spend together if Fyfe's friend didn't come up with something solid.

"I called him when Percy told me you'd taken James," Fyfe said.

"He told me. I should probably ask how you two know each other and why he seems to be working for you rather than for me and the conclave, but I don't think I want the answer to those questions."

"You're going to have them anyway. We met a few hundred years ago. We were lovers for a while, but we drifted apart. We've always stayed in contact, though, so I was glad when Maurice told me he was part of the team that was investigating James."

"Maurice? As in, the conclave member?"

Fyfe grinned. "Yeah, him. He's a friend, too."

James gently pulled on Fyfe's braid. "You're boasting," he murmured.

Fyfe pressed a kiss on the corner of James' lips. "I know, but for once, I don't care. I want Oren to know how well connected I am." He paused. "I *need* him to know."

It made sense. Fyfe was going to use everything and everyone he could to save James. How could James have doubted he was serious about him? He hadn't thought they could work. They were so different, in age and species, but he supposed they were both human at heart, and that was enough for them to connect. He'd kept himself out of the world for the past year, but that was over—if he made it out. He was going to be with Fyfe, make friends with Andrew, Faulkner, and even Aubrey. It didn't matter that Aubrey had dragged him all over the entrance of the coven's house. He'd been doing his job, and James was pretty sure he'd feel magnanimous if he was declared innocent and let go.

"As for why he's working for me," Fyfe continued. "Like I said, he's not. I called him and told him what James said about the situation he was in. I *did* ask him to investigate, but he would have done that anyway once he found out the case wasn't clear-cut like he'd thought."

"You sent him back to the pack." There was no accusation in Oren's voice, just curiosity, and maybe a touch of annoyance. He probably didn't like the fact that whatever Fyfe was saying, he *had* been doing his job for him.

"I asked him to make sure you guys weren't condemning an innocent to death. That's all. The fact that it was me asking didn't have anything to do with Ignatius' decision to go."

Oren looked around and sighed. His shoulders relaxed, and James hoped that meant good things. "All right. Since we have to wait for Ignatius to get here, why don't the two of you who are hurt come with me? I'll show you to the infirmary."

Andrew and Falkner looked at Fyfe, who nodded and told them, "Go. I'll sit here with James."

"I'll stay, too," Aubrey said.

James was surprised, but he knew he shouldn't be. Aubrey was loyal to Fyfe, and *that* wasn't surprising.

Fyfe grinned. "What if I wanted to have a proper reunion with James?"

Oren pointed a finger at him. "No sex in my interrogation room." He left with Andrew and Falkner in tow.

James didn't want to do anything except snuggle closer to Fyfe and take comfort in his presence. There would be plenty of time for questions later, and if there wasn't, well, he didn't want to use his last moment with Fyfe to ask them anyway.

Fyfe ran a hand through James' hair. "Are you okay? They didn't rough you up, did they?"

"I'm fine. I'd be better if I was back home with you, though."

Fyfe kissed James' forehead. "Soon, pup."

James decided to believe him, since it wouldn't do him any good to obsess over what would happen to him.

They were still huddled together when the door opened again. James wasn't sure how much time had passed, but it had felt like forever. Fyfe straightened, and James wondered if he was going to ask him to get off his lap. He didn't, but James slid down anyway when he saw one of the three men who walked in. "Oscar?"

He looked bad. He was pale, so pale James wondered if he might faint. He smiled weakly, and James moved toward him. He stopped before he could round the table though. The second man, the only one he didn't know, wrapped his arm around Oscar's waist and stared at James. James had no idea who it was, although he suspected it was Ignatius. That didn't explain why he seemed so protective of Oscar, but James wasn't going to poke the bear, not when the bear was the one who would keep his head on his shoulders.

"Hey, James. Still in trouble, huh?" Oscar asked.

"As you can see. Are you okay?"

"I've been better, but I'll be okay."

Ignatius helped Oscar lower himself into the chair opposite the one Fyfe and James had occupied. Fyfe waited until Oscar was sitting down to grab his friend and wrap him into his arms. "It's good to see you, Igni."

Ignatius glared, but he patted Fyfe's shoulder. "Don't call me that. And I can't believe you only call me when you need help, asshole."

Fyfe moved away. "I could say the same for you." His gaze flickered to Oscar. "Have you told him?"

"Yes. We'll talk about that later, though."

Oren cleared his throat. "Ignatius? Care to enlighten me on what you found? We'll talk about the fact that you went rogue on me later."

James hoped that didn't mean Ignatius would have problems with the conclave. Oren didn't look angry, but he wasn't the one in charge.

Ignatius nodded. "When Fyfe called me and asked me to look into this, he told me Oscar was the one who freed James the first time we got him. Since we hadn't talked to him at all when we were with the pack, I decided to do it. I thought he had to have a good reason to let James go, and I was right."

"He didn't do anything," Oscar said, his voice tight. "My father did."

Oren walked around the table and sat in front of Oscar. "Can you tell me what happened?"

James went to stand behind Oscar, next to Ignatius. Oscar had been his only friend when he'd been with the pack. They hadn't been able to be open about it, but they'd been close, and James hated that Oscar had been hurt because of him. The least he could do was offer him his silent support, and he didn't even care if it earned him a glare from Ignatius.

"My father was the pack's beta. He's been the beta for decades, and he'd been talking about becoming alpha one day more often every year. I didn't pay attention to it when I was a kid, but as I grew up, I saw how cruel he was. I also knew right from the beginning that he was plotting against Alpha Torres." Oscar bit his lower kip. "I tried to tell him, but my father beat me."

Fyfe tightened his hands. He wanted to wrap them around that beta's throat and squeeze until he stopped breathing. The man had hurt his own son as well as James, and Fyfe couldn't accept that. If the conclave didn't do anything, he would.

"I wasn't able to tell Alpha Torres what was going on. When nothing happened, I thought my father had decided it wasn't worth it, or that maybe he didn't have the guts to go through with it." Oscar chuckled darkly. "I should have known better. He was just waiting for the perfect scapegoat."

"And he got me," James said.

"Yes. He—he found out you and I were friends. I think that's one of the reasons he decided to put this on you. I'm sorry, James."

James gently patted Oscar's shoulder. "Don't worry about it. This wasn't your fault, only your father's."

Oscar nodded. "I know." He turned his attention back to Oren. "He killed Alpha Torres. I wasn't there when he did it, but I know he did because he talked about how he'd set James up for it and how James was going to be killed. He hates James because he's a bitten wolf. I know you might not believe me, but—"

"I do," Oren interrupted. "And since Ignatius was away for so long, I suspect he gathered evidence."

Ignatius nodded. "I did. I talked to Oscar and several other pack members. Oscar's father wasn't happy about it, but since I'm a conclave enforcer, he couldn't say no." Ignatius hesitated. "He doesn't know I left yet, or that I took Oscar with me. He whipped him when he found out what he'd done, and he was going to sell him to a nearby pack who wanted a born wolf."

Oren pinched the bridge of his nose. "Dammit. Okay. Oscar, you're at least eighteen, right?"

"Yes."

"Then your father doesn't have a say in this. You're here of your own free will?"

"Yes."

"And he's going to become one of my coven members," Fyfe said. Oren probably needed to know. He wanted to ask Ignatius what he wanted, but doing that in front of Oren wasn't the best idea.

Oren arched a brow. "He is?"

"As is James, actually. Because you're going to let him go, right?"

"I am. They're both wolves, though."

"I'm aware of that, and since I'm the only one who has a say in who is or isn't a coven member, it doesn't matter." Fyfe had always hated that power, but right now, he was happy he had it. He was going to have to find and get rid of the other snitch in his coven, but once that was done, he was pretty sure no one would mind the wolves. They might take a little while getting used to it, but they'd make things work. Fyfe was sure of it. "And now that you know where you can find both of them, we'll be going."

Fyfe grabbed James' hand and dragged him toward the door. He hoped Oren wasn't going to try to stop them. He wanted to go home and get into bed with his man, and he wanted that to happen now.

"Fyfe?" Ignatius called out.

Fyfe sighed. "Yes?"

"I have to stay and talk to Oren." Ignatius looked down at Oscar.

Fyfe melted. He didn't think he'd ever seen his friend look so smitten with anyone, not even with himself. "We'll take care of him, I promise. And once you're done here, just come to the house. You can have a guest room for as long as you need one." Fyfe hoped it would become a permanent room, but he didn't say that in front of Oren. That was for Ignatius to explain, not for him.

They picked up Andrew and Falkner from the infirmary on their way out. They both looked at Oscar with curiosity, but thankfully, they didn't ask who he was or what was going on. Fyfe had had enough questions for today, and he was going to have to order a gathering of all coven members tomorrow anyway. He didn't want to have to explain himself twice.

Oscar looked a little lost without Ignatius, and Fyfe's heart broke for him, but he was glad when Aubrey gently touched Oscar's arm and steered him toward the stairs. Fyfe mouthed *thank-you* at him, and Aubrey rolled his eyes and shrugged. Fyfe was going to have to give him a promotion or something — he wasn't sure what, but he'd find out.

"God, it's good to be back," James said.

"It's good to have you back." Fyfe pulled him into their bedroom and closed the door. "None of your stuff is here, but you won't need it tonight."

James cocked his head. "I won't?"

"No. You'll be naked in just a few minutes, and you'll stay naked until tomorrow. I'll text Ignatius to go to Percy's place and grab your bag. Or maybe Richie. I don't know, and right now, I don't care. I just want you naked and in my bed."

James laughed. "I should probably shower first."

"Don't. I want your scent." Fyfe swallowed. "I thought I'd lost you."

James' expression softened. "You didn't."

"And I never will, because I'm not letting you out of my sight ever again." Fyfe unbuttoned his shirt and let it drop on the floor. "Naked, pup. Now."

Fyfe didn't have to repeat it. Clothes flew as he and James shed them, and he didn't give James time to say anything once they got into bed. He grabbed him and pulled him close, plastering their bodies together and kissing him as if it was the last time he could do it.

It nearly had been, and Fyfe could still feel the deep-seated fear that he'd lose the love of his life. He wasn't going to tell James that because he didn't want to freak him out, but he hoped he'd never feel that way again.

They rolled until James was under Fyfe. Fyfe looked down at him, and he could see his entire world in James' eyes, his present and his future, his everything. He leaned down to kiss him, and things slowed down. They weren't frantic anymore because they had forever.

They slid together, their skin smooth and slick. James wrapped his legs around Fyfe, trusting him not to take more than he was ready to offer.

"I was so scared," James murmured.

"You don't need to be, not anymore. I'll take care of you."

James rolled his eyes. "I don't need you to."

"But I will anyway, just like you'll take care of me." He kissed James again. He wanted James to forget what had happened today and what *could* have happened. He wanted him to focus on what was going on in their bed right now and nothing else.

Fyfe kissed down James' throat, pausing at his nipples to lick and suck them. James was reacting in all the right ways, writhing under Fyfe and trying to pull him close. Fyfe didn't let him, though. He moved down, kissing his way to James' groin, making sure to take his time. James' moans and pleas were music to his ears, and he'd never heard anything so sweet.

He pressed James' hips to the mattress with both hands and wrapped his lips around the head of James' cock. James swore and tried to thrust, but Fyfe didn't let him move. He liked having James at his mercy like this, and he was going to take advantage of it. He'd learned a lot about sex during his long life, and it was all for this moment.

Fyfe teased James with light touches and licks until he was begging for more. Fyfe's own cock felt like it was about to burst, and he needed more. He needed James around him or inside him, but he knew neither of them would last long enough to get through prep. He did the next best thing, surging up and capturing James' lips with his, tangling their tongues together as they wrapped their bodies together.

It was messy and damp, but it was perfect. They both thrust against each other, desperate in their frantic search for pleasure and completion. It felt like the beginning of something, a life together, a love so vast that Fyfe didn't think he'd ever felt anything like it. It was a promise of more when they came almost at the same time, clinging to each other so hard no one could have separated them.

Chapter Seven

James knew this was necessary, but that didn't mean he liked it. He didn't want Fyfe to have to kick anyone out of the coven. Fyfe had been betrayed, though, not once but twice, and he needed to act like the coven leader he was.

That role made James slightly uncomfortable. Fyfe had assured him that morning that he wouldn't have to do anything, even though they were together. The coven didn't have a role for the leader's lover, and that wouldn't change even with James moving in with them. James wasn't so sure of that, though.

It was obvious that the coven looked up to Fyfe. Even now that they didn't know what was happening, why Fyfe had convened them and why he was in the living room with two werewolves and an unknown vampire, they didn't look scared. A few were wary and stayed far away from James and Oscar, but that was the worst reaction James had seen so far.

He was sitting next to Fyfe on the couch, with Ignatius and Oscar on a second couch. Aubrey, Andrew, and Falkner were there too, the last two worse for wear but seemingly okay. James wasn't sure how he'd be able to thank them, but he had time to think about it, since he wasn't going anywhere.

He still had a hard time believing he was a coven member now. He'd never felt at home with the pack, no matter how hard he'd tried, but even though the coven members didn't know about him yet, he'd lived there a few weeks, and he knew this was home for him. It didn't matter that almost everyone was a vampire. He didn't care about that. He thought the hatred between the two species was ridiculous, but of course, he'd only been a werewolf for a year.

"Thank you for coming," Fyfe said. He looked regal, sitting on the couch, wearing a white shirt and dress pants. His many tattoos were barely visible under the fabric, but James knew they were there. He'd spent enough time tracing them with his fingers and tongue to know them.

Fyfe's heavy braid hung over his shoulder, and he looked at every coven member for a moment. His gaze stopped on one of the elders, and James knew the moment had come. He held his breath as Fyfe said, "As you can see, James is back, and he's here to stay. I know not all of you believe in having a mixed coven, and you're welcome to come talk to me later today or tomorrow, or any time you have a problem. We'll try to work things out together. But I can't abide or accept traitors. I thought I'd made that clear when I asked Alfred to leave, yet someone else here betrayed me. Someone called the conclave and told them where to find James."

"What do you mean?" a woman asked. James wished he'd spent more time outside Fyfe's bedroom when he'd been there. He didn't know anyone but Aubrey, Andrew, and Falkner.

Fyfe took James' hand and linked their fingers together. "James was accused of something he didn't do. The conclave was after him, and I offered him to stay with us so they wouldn't catch him. We fell in love."

"You knew he was a killer and you let him stay here?" the elder responsible for James' capture asked. James didn't know how old she was, but Fyfe had told him she'd been close to Alfred. A few others had been as well, but they'd distanced themselves from him when Fyfe had kicked him out. Odette had been the only one who'd come to Fyfe to ask him to be lenient.

He hadn't been, and he wasn't going to be this time, either.

Fyfe's expression hardened. "Didn't you hear it when I said he was innocent?"

"You couldn't be sure of that."

"Maybe not, but I was right, wasn't I? And if you had doubts about James, you should have come to me instead of calling the conclave. Or was that revenge for kicking Alfred out?"

There were a few gasps, and the few people standing with Odette took steps back, dissociating themselves from her dramatically. James wanted to roll his eyes at the gesture, but those people were afraid Fyfe was going to bunch them together. James understood that.

Odette smartly didn't say anything. She had to know what was going to happen. Everyone in the room did.

"Odette, you have two hours to pack your things and leave the coven. You're not welcome here anymore," Fyfe declared.

"You have no right," she spat out.

"But I do. Or did you forget I'm the leader?"

"You should never have been."

"Probably not. I didn't *want* to be. But I got rid of your old leader, and I had to accept this job. That means that I have the right to welcome people into the coven or kick them out, which is what I'm doing with you." Fyfe leaned forward. "I've never asked for much from you and the others, but loyalty is the one thing I don't compromise on. You should go pack, Odette. Aubrey will come with you to help you and make sure you make it out the door in time."

James almost expected Odette to continue protesting, especially after she looked around for support, but she seemed to understand what everyone else already knew. She wasn't going to get help because they all knew she'd done the wrong thing.

Fyfe waited until she and Aubrey had left the room to smile. "Now that this is over, I have more news. Again, what I said before still stands. If you have any kind of doubts or fears, come talk to me. Don't do what Odette and Alfred did. I want our coven to succeed and for every single one of you to be safe and happy. Having so many people live in the same house doesn't make it easy, but I do believe we *can* make it work."

"Just come out with it," Falkner said.

Fyfe glared at him, and Falkner stuck his tongue out. James pressed his lips together. Even if the rest of the coven never accepted him, he wouldn't be alone. He'd have Andrew and Falkner, Oscar, and Aubrey.

And of course, Fyfe.

"As you all know, James and I are together, and he's going to become a coven member. He is *not* dangerous, whatever Odette and Alfred might have told you. He's working with another wolf to get his own under control, and I'll make sure he's secure during the full moon, so you don't have to worry about that. Oscar here is also a werewolf and will also become a coven member. He doesn't have control problems, as he's a born werewolf." Fyfe smiled at him, and Oscar tentatively smiled back. James hoped he'd be happy here. He deserved it.

"And finally, Ignatius is a vampire and a conclave enforcer. He won't live here full time right away since his job takes him all over the country, but I asked him to become a coven member, and he agreed. I hope everyone will find a way to live together in peace. I won't tolerate anything like what happened with Odette and Alfred again. You're free to leave now."

Fyfe leaned against James, and James let him. He knew

Fyfe was conflicted between looking accessible and weak, but he didn't care about any of that. He doubted anyone else would have anything to say about the way Fyfe had acted. Besides, they were together. He'd just made that public. None of his coven members would be surprised or would care if Fyfe and James cuddled, so James wrapped an arm around Fyfe's shoulder and pulled him close to kiss his temple.

"That went well, right?" Fyfe asked.

"I think so."

"As long as Odette doesn't go crazy, this will be over soon." Fyfe smiled at James. "And I can't wait to have you in bed again."

James laughed. "That's going to have to wait."

"Why?"

"You don't think everyone is going to want to talk to you about this? They just got three new coven members and lost two over a few days. Even if they don't care that Oscar and I are werewolves, they're going to have things to say and questions to ask, and your job is to answer them."

Fyfe groaned. "But I don't want to. I want to spend the next week in bed with you and not think about anything else."

James couldn't promise an entire week—Fyfe had too many responsibilities for that—but he *could* organize something. "How about we spend the few days after the full moon there? I'll organize everything. You just need to make sure someone else is in charge while we're on vacation."

Fyfe grinned. "I know there was a reason I loved you."

"Only one?"

Fyfe's smile softened, and it told James everything he needed to know. "One thousand."

YOU MAY ALSO ENJOY THE FOLLOWING FROM EXTASY BOOKS INC:

Sasha
Catherine Lievens

Excerpt

Sasha slid the beer over the counter and nodded at the woman. She grinned at him and leaned closer, exposing more of her cleavage. "Thank you."

He smiled at her and turned. She was cute, but so not his type. She didn't have a dick.

"Hey man."

Sasha turned toward the next customer, his smile widening when he saw Grey. "Hey." Sasha touched his hair, making sure it was still in place, and he got closer. "What can I do for you?"

Grey waved toward a spot behind him. "There's a group of us tonight."

"How many beers?"

Grey chucked. "You know us so well."

"It's my job."

"I don't know. I thought I was more than a job for you." He pressed his hand to his chest. "You wound me, Sasha."

Sasha rolled his eyes. "Are you going to order? Because as

you can see, the place is packed, and I have other customers." Sasha wouldn't have dared to speak like that to customers, but Grey wasn't only that. Sasha considered him a
friend, kind of, and he knew that went for Grey, too. They
didn't hang out much, but that was more because Sasha
tended to isolate himself, even from friends.

Grey gave Sasha his order. Sasha wished he could go over
to the table Grey shared with his friends and sit with them,
but it was Friday night, and he wouldn't be able to take his
break for a while. Still, he couldn't look away as Grey
grabbed the beer bottles and left with a nod. He was there
with his mate and a few other people, and Sasha's gaze went
straight to Hunter.

He knew he shouldn't be staring. He knew he shouldn't
even be thinking about Hunter. There was no way Hunter
would ever want to take him back to the bathroom like he
did so often with other guys, and Sasha didn't want that.
No, Sasha had given up love. He didn't deserve it. But damn
if he didn't miss it.

He shook his head. The only reason he was missing it was
because he hadn't been enough, and he wasn't going to
make that mistake again. Besides, even if he wanted to,
Hunter had never given him a second glance, and that was
okay.

He might be Sasha's type—or rather, he was anyone's
type, with that long, blond hair and those mischievous
eyes—but Sasha had never been into playboys. Hunter had a
different guy with him every time he came to the bar, and
when he didn't have one, he found one on the premises.
Sasha had always hated being a notch on a belt, even when
he'd been a college kid.

It hadn't changed.

"How are things going?" Nate asked, slipping behind the
bar.

Sasha pressed his lips together. He wasn't going to smile.
"You're late."

"That's one of the perks of being the boss."

"I should ask for a raise. You've abandoned me to the crowd without a second thought."

Nate laughed and punched Sasha's shoulder. "Shut up. You're more than able to wrangle them."

"Doesn't mean I wouldn't rather have help."

Nate patted Sasha's shoulder. "You have it now, so stop complaining and get back to work."

Sasha did. It was easy to lose himself in the steady rhythm of taking orders, handing out drinks, and taking money. This was his job. He did it almost every night, and he didn't have to focus on it anymore.

"Hey, pretty," a man drawled.

Sasha suppressed a sigh. "What can I get you?"

"How about your phone number?"

Sasha almost rolled his eyes, but he didn't want Nate to lose a customer because he couldn't keep his reactions to himself. "I meant to drink."

"Whatever you'll have."

"I'm working. I can't drink."

"I'm sure you can take a break and sit with me."

"I'm sorry."

Sasha turned to tell Nate to take the guys' order, but the man reached out, catching Sasha's long hair and pulling on it none too gently. "Come on, pretty boy. Show me what you're hiding under that hair, yeah?"

Sasha jerked back, and thankfully, the man let go of his hair. He'd seen, though. Sasha could tell by the horror on his face. He was ready to bet the asshole wasn't so eager to have a drink with him now.

"What the fuck is going on here?" Nate's voice boomed.

The man raised his hands. "Nothing. I was just ordering a drink."

"Sasha?"

From the look Nate gave him, he could tell there was more than that happening, but Sasha wasn't going to say anything. "I'm okay."

"You sure?"

"Yeah."

"Why don't you take your break now?"

Sasha risked a glance at the guy who'd touched him, and sure enough, he was looking everywhere but at him. He'd changed his mind as soon as he'd seen the scar.

Sasha didn't blame him. He knew it was ugly. He was mostly used to it by now, but sometimes, especially first thing in the morning, it still made him jolt when he saw himself in the mirror. "I can work."

Nate glared at the man who was now ignoring them. "Take your break. It's only fair since you had to deal with the crowd on your own until now."

Sasha wasn't going to refuse twice. He didn't think it was necessary, but it was a relief, even though he was used to people's reactions when they first saw his scar. Some pitied him, some were disgusted. Most didn't know where to look or how to behave as if the scar changed who he was as a person, as if it made him not quite human.

He nodded. "Okay. Thanks."

"Take your time. Have something to eat. The crowd isn't going anywhere."

Sasha took his apron off and left the area behind the bar. He looked straight ahead, just in case the man who'd touched him was looking at him, but he doubted he would. He wasn't as pretty as he'd seemed to be, and that was what that man had been after — a pretty face.

The hallway leading to the break room was quieter than the bar, but not by much. Sasha looked down, his hair sliding in front of him and hiding his scar, just in case someone came out of the bathroom while he was there. He managed to slip into the break room without encountering anyone, though.

He closed the door and leaned back against it, taking a deep breath and closing his eyes.

He was okay. He was always okay. The scar was just that—a scar. He didn't care about it, except because of the way it made people look at him—and for what it reminded him of. He still had nightmares about that day, and he always would. He couldn't forget, not when the reminder was so obvious on his face—and when he'd lost some of his vision because of the wound that had caused the scar.

He swallowed and opened his eyes. He saw well enough, even with his compromised eye. He could work and live normally—something he'd always felt he didn't deserve.

He shook his head. He had to stop doing this. He couldn't think about Cedric right now, not if he wanted to be able to finish his shift. He needed to finish it, because he needed the tips to pay rent and buy food. He'd have the time to cry once he was home, alone in his bed.

But first, food.

Sasha opened his locker and got out the sandwich he'd brought from home. He knew he could go to the kitchen and ask Lydia to whip something up for him, but she was busy with the customers, and he didn't want to take her away from that. He could get some fries when the evening started winding down, and people left the bar. He was in no hurry to go back to the crowd out there, and he hoped Nate wouldn't mind it if he spent a bit more time in the break room.

Sometimes, quiet time was all that got him through the night.

About the Author

Catherine lives in Italy, country of good food and hot men. She used to write fantasy as a child, but it was reading her first gay erotic romance novel that made her realize that that was what she really wanted to write.

After graduating from college in English language and translation, she divides her day between writing, reading, taking care of her son and reading some more.

You can find her on Facebook and Twitter or on her website: authorcatherinelievens.wordpress.com

Email: lievens.catherine@gmail.com

Newsletter: http://eepurl.com/c-uvKn